ECCENTRIC CIRCLES

◇◇◇

ECCENTRIC CIRCLES

Larry Duberstein

THE PERMANENT PRESS

to Flora and Martin
(and with special thanks to Ted and Dale)

Library of Congress Cataloging-in-Publication Data

Duberstein, Larry.
    Eccentric Circles / by Larry Duberstein.
      p. cm.
    ISBN 1-877946-20-6
    I. Title.
    PS3554.U253E28   1992
    813'.54—dc20   90-40188
                                  CIP

Manufactured in the United States of America

THE PERMANENT PRESS
Noyac Road
Sag Harbor, NY 11963

CONTENTS

The Second Craziest Person in Casper, Wyoming

I knew something was wrong with this picture even before I opened the front door. Groping past all the junk in Holly's dark hallway I half expected a nice smack on the head—though I was also thinking, False alarm you paranoid weirdo, you took one too many drugs in the last fiscal year.

There was something, though, there was a girl on the bed asleep. And as my buddy Wayne said when I told him this whole tale, a strange girl in your bed is not necessarily a *bad* dream.

Now it was not my bed precisely, if I do generally sleep in it. (With Holly. It's her bed.) And it wasn't exactly a strange girl either, as it turned out. I didn't know when I first took her in, saw just the naked back with kind of a sweet twist to it. Then I saw the blonde hair and that old blue coat of hers on the chair and knew it was Melinda.

So you could say that yes it was a strange girl after all, just not a girl I didn't already know. Or for that matter hadn't fancied once or twice in the past, though of course who doesn't fancy Melinda Daniels might be a better question to ask, since apart from her slim and pretty looks she also happens to be the sort of girl who'll come right in your window and be sleeping naked in your bed.

Right: Holly's window, Holly's bed. But still. I used to go out to the quarter horses with her friend Booth back in the old days, as far back as ol Jimmy Carter. My friend at the time (Fawn, she called herself, though really it was Edna) knew the two of them, and so we four would eat together, do cookouts and beer blasts and so forth, play some cards. One of those couple deals where after a certain amount of it you start to wonder if you wouldn't rather leave with the other one instead of your own. Just for a while, you know, for the sheer hell of it or for a change. Plus of course it was Melinda.

I decided the thing to do was make a joke of it. Climb in bed and act surprised: Hey what the hell, you're not Holly, what's the deal here? So I strip down and start to peel back the quilt when I uncover her damned infant Clayton in there alongside her. I forgot the kid existed (which he *didn't* exist a short while back) plus she looked so slim and single lying there.

By the time she woke to the scuffling, I had scrambled my ass back in my jeans. Melinda turned herself over nice as you please, not caring about breasts particularly, so that I was obliged to pretend I didn't care either until she shook her head clear and yanked up the quilt.

"Pete," she said. "Hi. Hope I didn't throw you off."

"Not you. Ol Clayton did, though."

"Isn't he sweet? Look at the little toad sleep through everything. He always does."

"He's a good boy, for sure."

"Well I'm sorry about just showing up here. I would have asked first—"

"I know that."

"—but I knew Holl was in the hospital and I just guessed you'd be staying at your own place."

"I would, but the furnace blew out. I had someplace warm to go to, so I went. That's all it was."

"Same with me. Someplace warm to go."

"Furnace kick off at your house too?"

"No. No, it's me and Billy. You know I told him he had to find work? I told him before the baby came and that's almost two years by now. So I finally took some action."

"Just now? Tonight?"

"You got it. I used the window in back."

"I figured that. Just curious, though—did you leave Clayton on the ground and go back out for him, or did you bootleg him as you dove through?"

"Neither. I put him in first and came on after. He stands up, you know. He can *walk*, Pete."

"Just curious."

"So do you think it would be a problem, my staying here a short while?"

"I don't see why, as long as you're willing to sleep with me."

"You mean sleep, or *sleep*?"

"Hell, Melinda, I don't mean a damn thing, I was only joking," I told her, though I'd tell you her eyes looking up right then were the most beautiful thing I'd seen in my life.

"Oh."

"But what about Bill? Isn't Bill going to mind?"

That was perfectly stupid because of course he'd mind. If he didn't mind, she wouldn't have done it in the first place. She was trying to make a point with him. But apart from being knocked silly by the sight of her, I was trying to find things out, too. Joke or no joke, what if I *could* sleep with Melinda?

It's not like I lack the capacity for a little evil. The week Holl was away in Denver, I ended up in bed with the girl in the red dress at Booth's party and it wasn't a case of I didn't love Holl or did love the other girl in her red dress or out of it. It's just that as I say I can be capable of a sin, the same as you can. Same as we all can, by my calculations, with the possible exception always of Ed Hightower.

So maybe I began wondering if Melinda wasn't capable too. At the very least I knew she was famous for her massages, and I could end up needing one of those, for having been displaced onto the sofa-bed by her and Clayton Royal. But a girl who will come in the window might very well sleep with you and surely she will give you a nice little back rub if she doesn't. Which she did: the back rub.

"Who cares what he minds," she told me. "A man who won't feed his own son? Does he seem to care what *I* mind?"

"So you won't care if he does mind."

"That's true. But Billy minding and not minding is beside the point. Holly would mind."

"What about you, though?"

"I wouldn't mind."

"But Holly would."

"Is that supposed to be a joke? Hollywood?"

"No."

"Well you know for sure she would mind. But I suppose I could rub your back for you, if you want."

The next night it was Bill who came in the window. Not many secrets in this town.

After I got off work, and after dinner (which Melinda and I shared in Holl's kitchen, just your basic bacon and scrambled eggs), we drove up to the hospital together. I'd planned on going every night and Melinda planned on going sometime, so there we were. And there was Bill when we got back.

We took Holly flowers and magazines and some chocolate she could squirrel away for ammunition. She was looking good and not a bit scared of the operation either. They had said it was a routine procedure—back home in a jiffy, back to work in two weeks—and Holl was never much of a worrier in the first place. I myself do some serious worrying anytime I am *near* a hospital and when it comes my turn to get committed to the inside of one for a little razorwork, they won't need a drop of painkiller because I'll go in a coma first.

Holl got the simple truth on Melinda moving in at Price Street. The sofa-bed story was good by her, as a non-worrier anyway. With ol Clayton there it didn't strike her as a threat, I guess. Or maybe she did under-rate me, that's possible too.

Now I wasn't surprised to find Bill at the apartment but it was a whole new confusion to see Melinda greet him with a loving hug and hello and say how glad she was to see him. Because of course she could have been seeing him every minute if she hadn't moved out. But here Bill was as sweet on the little boy as he secretly wished to be on her, sort of misdirecting his interest as a trick to court Melinda.

Lord knows why it never crossed my dull mind the night before, since it worked like one powerful charm. She just started *shining* on ol Billy as he cheered Clayton Royal along. And the merrier Clayton became, running and giggling, the more lit up his mother, until I was afraid she might jump Bill before my eyes. I could just feel her softly falling.

It was done politely, though, after a lengthy tuck-in for the baby, and a few pops of the bottle Bill brought, and good-nights all around. Nonetheless it was surely done, because I damn well heard it done, mooing and moaning in Holly's bed till I nearly chose to go back home to the deep freeze.

In the morning it didn't mean a thing. Then they went and had the fight I had expected last night, with Bill saying enough of this shit and let's go home, and Melinda saying call me when you found steady work, bub, and not before, and Bill going crazy for not grasping her logic, and Melinda advising him to put his logic where the sun don't shine even in a nudist colony. In the end Bill was throwing things that belonged to Holly, so I was forced to interrupt them.

Things calmed right down to a reasonable back-and-forth (had he looked for work here and weren't they said to be hiring there) but I did finally have to get my own ass to work. "Will I expect to find the lot of you here tonight, then?" I asked them, thinking if so I might prefer to see how the burner was coming along at my place. I couldn't get an answer (as they truly didn't know one yet themselves) so that is what I did do and was delighted to find the heat chugging along full throttle again. We went below zero that night and next day in the fields, and I personally hate that degree of cold. No amount of clothes gets it done for me at ten below zero.

So who knows what they did about it. I kept to my own track the next few days. They performed the operation and Holl came through all right; she was pale and weak but that was to be expected, they said. Then they told us that as well as it had gone with her, they would need to go back in again and at that even Holl was scared pissless. As for me, I knew. I was *sure* I was going to lose her. But as anyone who has accompanied me to the quarter horses can tell you, not all my hunches are letter perfect, and I didn't lose her, she came through fine both times.

A few nights after the second procedure, her color was back, and her energy, and she was threatening to dance me across the floor in that solar room where you sit. I was relieved, damn happy, and stopped in at McCloud's on my way home for some beer and pinball, just to celebrate things swinging back toward normal.

Normal, hell. Two hours later, around midnight, Melinda and Clayton Royal showed up at *my* place.

"Bunk here tonight?" she said.

"Holl's house burn down or something?"

"No but Billy's moved in there now. He won't stay off, Pete."

"So here you are."

"Always on the go," she grinned. If you are thinking why the hell not just send her packing, with all this crazy shit plus the little guy yelling his head off, well it's because you don't realize what a pretty creature she is. Pretty can count. Besides which I was not particularly enjoying my total loneliness in certain respects.

"I don't want you to misunderstand," she said—yet said it with that look of hers, such that I was thinking maybe I *should* misunderstand. Melinda has better pals than me, so what's she doing here? It's one thing coming in Holly's back window, another thing coming in my front door. No?

"Won't Bill just come over here?"

"Not right off the bat. He won't think of here, you see." (That was it.) "But if he does, I'd sure appreciate your saying you haven't seen us."

"Lie to him?"

"Yes, please."

"And then what? Stuff a rag in Clayton's mouth? Hell, Melinda, this starts to get weird."

"I know it."

"I guess you can stay, and I might even lie for you, but this time you really will have to sleep with me."

Did I mean it? Well no, not seriously: not that I'd stick to it if she opted out into the cold. Let's say I meant it as a serious *suggestion*. And if it seems illogical on top of my telling how much I loved Holly, it honestly wasn't. I could have bedded with Melinda anytime in the last eight years, happily, and still loved my Holl. Now with both the past and the future looking pretty damn distant for me, sexually speaking, the immediate present seemed a good time to tide me over.

"Maybe," she said.

"How will you tell?"

"Maybe tomorrow. Tonight at this hour is just not a live option for me, Pete. Even if the little man was not as miserable as he clearly is."

"But tomorrow, you think."

"Maybe. On the complete sly from everyone? Why not?"

I couldn't believe her too much. If you are looking for positive signs, you can't really be too encouraged by 'why not.' She did say it, though, I had to respect the fact, so I poked my head in the next morning before work.

"It's tomorrow, Melinda."

Sitting there in a pretty white cotton slip, with her hair pinned up in a cloud, she didn't know what in hell I meant.

"Don't you remember? Why not tomorrow?"

"Oh I know it, Pete," she said now, cocking her smile at baby Clayton as if to say ain't *this* situation too bad. "It must not be tomorrow yet, if you see what I mean."

I didn't see, not yet. That night I climbed down off the rig, went home to clean up (no sign of Melinda there) and then straight up to the hospital. A promise is a promise. Not that I was sorry, either, because Holl and I had our usual fun, we were happy, and I could tell myself *here's* why not, I love this girl, dammit.

And yet without unloving her in the slightest, I was most definitely leaning back the other way at McCloud's—back in the direction of why not. I mean, since it's a freebie and much needed, plus on the sly from everyone? But don't ever let anyone tell you the human isn't one strange animal. If he thinks so, well he's just the last to know, that's all.

Meanwhile Melinda was of course not there. Wherever the wind had blown her this time, she was not a girl to plan on. I waited anyway. She had my spare key and so I waited for her, just the way a young fool would have (and I may be a fool but I am way past young, I am a thirty-two year fool to be precise) and I kept waiting past two a.m. for steps or a key clattering.

At that point I dressed and spun over to Price Street, partly to see who was living there by now. No one was. They had left it a mess but I crawled in Holly's bed and slept there, for the simple reason that at home I knew I would just keep listening for Melinda, even though I also knew she wasn't coming. No one goes anyplace at that hour in zero degrees.

I overslept reveille, slept beautifully as a matter of fact, and decided to blow off work with a telephone lie. Possibly go bet on some ponies instead. For some crazy reason

I was in a good mood, but I guess crazy reasons are all there is. I straightened up at Holl's, scrubbed the pots and swept the breakage, and sealed off the smelly diapers I found floating in the trash. Then, for the sheer whimsical hell of it, I dialed Melinda's own telephone, and got her.

"Can you talk?"

"Sure," she told me.

"I mean, is Bill there, now."

"Billy? Nuh uh. But he will be back later if you—"

"I mean *hell*, Melinda, did you forget *all* about last night? Forget I was still alive?"

Saying it that way also supplied me with the answer. Sure she did. Completely. I had outlived my usefulness— though I sometimes wonder what would have happened if I hadn't outlived it quite so soon.

"Absolutely not, Pete. I was going to let you know soon as I could."

"Know what, you spaceshot?"

"That things are working out. Bill got hired in Glenrock and things are really looking up."

"What a difference a day makes."

"I know it. I hope you understand—"

"I hope I don't, Melinda. I couldn't take it if I were to start understanding you. But that's all right, that's fine."

I didn't go to the racetrack, drove up to the airfield instead, and don't ask me why or why not. I do like the amount of sky out there, the way the sky makes a kind of endless circle inside the mountains. They let you go up in the tower if you want and watch from behind glass panels. You can sit and drink your bottle of beer and no one will know you are the second craziest person in town. No one knows that in the midst of all this recent insanity, you are out here making decisions you'll never argue with again for the length of your pisspoor life.

To start with, put a damn lock on Holly's back window right away, absolutely, should have done it long ago. But then it hardly matters about that if you are saying yes to Holly, you are ready to go to the church with her, and yes to a baby too if they finally do clear her. Dump the his-and-hers, lock stock and windowlock, and start paying on something halfway nice with both our names on it.

There's just no point going anywhere else, however big the sky, and no point waiting any longer either, if you are thirty-two already and you know it's really love.

The Collected Letters

Doug had a twinge of self-consciousness taking over a booth designed to seat four. He needed the space, though, the sheltered bay, and was comfortable enough with his bowl of chips, his beer, and all Kate's letters arranged on the table.

Since yesterday, when he found the last of these leaning between balusters on the stairwell, Doug had been trying to shake his head clear, to regain his balance. Today he called in sick, then lay in bed like pure weight till one and walked all afternoon, but his mind kept whirling uselessly, temporarily out of order. Now he was here with the letters.

He had read them straight through in sequence a week ago and had done it twice last night. He would just have to keep on doing it until he got his damn strings tight.

Darling,

I've been here two days and already I want to forget the whole idea and come running home. I feel like such a cliché. New York is a bad dream, but like all day? I wonder how I ever decided to do this and I have not gone one single minute (as in literal minute, sixty seconds) without seeing you in my mind.

I was so sure it was Necessary and Right for me, and so here I sit in my "large studio apartment" with zero (count 'em, zero!) windows and nothing much else either. I hate TV but I'm thinking better get one quick or I'll be going for crazy.

People here won't talk to you. They won't talk to me, anyhow, maybe they'd talk to you. The streets are glutted with these people who won't smile or talk and the cars all try to run the people over (which may be why the people look so angry?) plus it smells like the inside of a muffler. Not that I've been in one, but the mind travels, you know.

That's the story line so far. Ambitious young fool of a girl gets the big cold shoulder from the cold hard city and wants to fly away home and yes, you told her so. I don't know how long I'll last. I miss you more than I even imagined, hate this place more than I imagined, hate myself a little too. Just one lonesome heartsick gal who wishes her man was here to laugh it all away with her.

All my love,
Katy

Doug was better now, much better. The table, the booth, the whole sweetly glowing room had become his den and he could smile at the funny signs ("In God We Trust—all others pay cash"), the stuffed blue-and-silver sailfish, yellowed photographs of F.D.R. and Carmen Basilio. He smiled at the flirty waitress, who was trying to peek at the second envelope. Something about her threw out a challenge to drink, and as she set him up with a mug of the house ale, Doug decided this must be the correct, ordained pace—a round for every letter.

When you were really depressed, according to Kate herself, you felt like a puppet whose strings had been cut.

But Doug was not depressed, he was in control of it now. The letters were all here, he had a world of time and space . . .

Darling,

You are not required to answer so promptly. If you do, you will waste your life, because I may very well write fifty-five letters a month. I'm neurotic, I need you, and I will write to sublimate, see? Whereas you are fine, you're home and happy (apart from the wandering bitch who *maybe* you miss in the evening when the sun go down) so save the trees.

You better not, by the way, I want tit for tat. (I know, I know, you just want tit, but I want fifty-five letters a month right back.)

Nothing new. I did see a movie last night with "one of the girls from the office" and it was fun just trying to have some fun. The movie was Bride of Rocky 6 or Son of Airport 7 and the popcorn cost as much as the movies do in Braxton. But the job feels a little better and I do know a few people there to say hello.

Have dreamed of you every night but the first (when I didn't sleep) and I daydream you too, every minute on the minute.

All my love,
Katy

There was something nice about having the letters in one neat packet, having every word together. It was a way of keeping Kate with him, a version of her. In the letters, particularly the early ones, she was perfectly herself, and her words were just a continuation of her voice, another chapter in their romance. Weeks after she'd left, Doug was able to feel that "in 'letter' and in spirit," as she put it, they were still together. Of course he knew now that even by the seventh or eighth letter, she would begin to sound different.

My love,

It is hard to believe I've been here just three weeks. A long dreary lifetime. Plus it feels like *you* have been away, not me, and I must confess that at times I've been a bit cross with you for deciding to go. Then I remember who's who and wonder if you are perhaps a bit cross with *me*. (I hope not.)

How are you? Cold and lonely in the night, I hope—but not really. I hope you're having some fun, because I won't even try to have any if I feel you aren't. There *are* ways of having fun here. New York is definitely better once you know your way around the streets, where to go for food etc. I've gotten close to a girl named Mary Davenport at the magazine. She's from Kansas, but has lived here six years, and has had a few actual writing assignments for the travel section. Imagine it. She got paid, lots too, for eating and sleeping in old-timey inns in Maine—checking out their log fires, coziness quotient and all that.

Anyhow, she's nice and a real help. In fact I may give up my glorious windowless studio and room with her. Her room-mate just married a doctor. I would pay less and have much more—four rooms of rent-controlled heaven, with a huge sunny kitchen.

Some bad news too. I won't be let out of jail till Thanksgiving. Apparently now is big push time at the magazine and one can't (CAN'T, says Mary) have any fun at all during sober October if one seeks to make ze favorable impression.

Maybe you would come down here? I am not sure what it would be like (since now I work most nights too). But *think* about it.

Much love,
Katy

"Are you writing a book?" asked the waitress, as she neatly centered his next ale on a round cardboard coaster. Each time she arrived, she brought a new coaster with a colorful painting of the Genessee 12-Horse Team pulling the old ale-wagon. Doug was collecting them in his shirt pocket.

"Hardly," said Doug, surprised to feel a wide grin stretching his features. "I'm just here getting hammered. Bombarded, as it were."

"So you are," she grinned back. "Or so it were."

"You have to admit, it's a lot easier than writing a fucking *book*."

"I'm sure it is. It just looked like you were a writer."

"No. I did have a girlfriend once who thought she was a writer, but that was at least a week ago."

"Oh," said the waitress, not so careless now, examining his face for symptoms. All she found was the grin, pinned up at both corners by ale, and so she went ahead with the banter. "I would never go out with a writer. You'd have to be so careful what you say."

"Plus you face the problem of who they get to play you in the movie version."

"Are you sure you're not a writer?"

"Pretty sure, but what's it matter? I haven't asked you out yet anyway."

She left him with his drink, his coaster, and a small

informative smile. Doug could tell his own smile was still too wide, but he couldn't seem to rein it in. He remembered the tough-guy line, Wipe that smile off your face, and gave it a try, to no avail.

Hey you, it's me again. Sorry I didn't write last week. They hitched the mule to the cart and didn't unhitch it till today, which happens to be Sunday. (Yes, I do know a girl cannot be a mule, or a mule cannot be a girl.) They have one of these crises every month, when it comes time to put an issue "to bed," and though I considered going mad from overwork, and from this crowded crazy town, I am a survivor as you know and don't go mad just casually. Really it was almost fun, with the "team" pulling together and all that rot. I guess all jobs are that way—whatever you do comes to seem important, it has to be done and done right in your one small corner of the universe, like a waiter taking care of his six tables. It is trivial, but only because everything is trivial when you boil it down.

I confess that NY is a bit contagious too. Once you stop fighting it, you do begin to feel a part of it all. I don't have that stranger-in-town complex any more. In fact, someone stopped me on the street to ask directions yesterday! What did I tell them? To hop in a taxi and give the address in a clear audible voice.

After the issue was safely tucked in last night, we had a minor celebration at the office. Mary got loopy on half a glass of champagne. Others drank a lot more and there was dancing, which only made me miss you. I didn't want to dance, and felt very alone—but being a survivor, I survived. And ended up practically carrying Mary back to the apartment. Which, by the way, is my main news. Were you perceptive enough to notice the new address on the envelope?

A gorgeous, placid Sunday. Even NY is quiet. Pretty and peaceful in Central Park, where the trees are turning. Some of the office crowd do a touch football game in the Park on Sundays, but I think I'll pass. (Get it?)

I trust you have been behaving yourself? *Miss* you.

Love,
Katy

Something wrong there, Doug mused absently, as he read the girlish postscript: "I have windows!" He had read this letter a month ago, read it last night, read it at noon today, and each time had found it painfully deflating— some intangible nameless horror hung from its margins— yet right now he could find it almost comforting. Something was missing, yes, but Katy did still love him. Plus the letter was part of a larger phenomenon, namely the collected letters, that continued to lend him a sense of control. He felt like a scholar scratching for the truth in the windless harbor of his book-plastered study.

But here was Donna—had he asked her name or had she volunteered it?—keeping him to her schedule. "You're rushing me. Do you work on commission in this place?"

"It isn't that sort of bar, sir," she laughed. Donna appeared to be having a high time of it and maybe she was; maybe she was part of the syndrome Kate had tried to define—people doing jobs, building their lives around those jobs, where on paper they were "just" the plumber, the bus driver, the waitress . . .

"That's an ugly word, isn't it?" he said. She stared at him amused and waiting. "Syndrome, I mean."

"I *knew* you were a writer. You are, aren't you?"

After she had gone again, he sipped slowly. The ale had lost its taste and bite, it was only cold, and he only kept drinking out of a mindless commitment to the occasion, to the place, to Donna herself.

The letters had lost some bite too, partly from being read too many times, so he let go of the determination to be absolutely thorough. Impatient with ransacking out clues and painful nuances, he skipped two dreary ones that were entirely concerned with the goddamned magazine, though at once he became less a scholar than a lawyer posthumously resolving the intricacies of his own last will and testament.

Douglas,

A first. I am writing you from the office. And typing the letter—hope you can stand being able to read it for a change. I guess I'm cheating the company, but hey, they owe me, and anyhow it's my only chance to do it, so clackety clickety click to you, sir.

Mid-autumn is gorgeous, even in NY. There is Central Park, of course, but there are also the rivers and smaller parks like Carl Schurz over by Gracie Mansion etc. And there is sometimes a real festival atmosphere, windy and bright, runners & rollerskaters, skateboarders and sailboaters, pretzelmen & pretzelwomen with their little carts and their cans of Sterno. A funny world, one day so sombre and the next day gay as a rainbow. Too much for a simple upstater like me.

Saturday we rented bicycles and rode till we were exhausted. Then a bunch of folks came by our place and we popped corn, so watching Mary's two-station TV was as good as a real movie, except for the ads. I was just so glad of a good Saturday. I thought of that song you like, about looking for the heart of Saturday night, and thought about you too, of course.

That's all the news fit to print in one coffee break. I thought your letter was too lovely, the long one I mean, and I plan to re-read it every time I get feeling the least bit insecure about my character, my intellect, or my physical charms. Thanks.

About phoning. Best bet is dinnertime Mon or Tues, or early Monday morning.

xox,
K.T.

Surprisingly, it was seven o'clock and the room had been filling up, someone at every other table, and Doug had to consider a move to the bar. He wobbled slightly getting untracked in the direction of the restroom and then, standing at the urinal, began to laugh, which caused him to sprinkle his shoes. "Perfectiy sober, officer," he said to his reflection in the mirror, then pushed back through the swinging door and dodged a waitress carrying drinks.

The booth bobbed up in his viewfinder like a small wooden ship, so alluring and safe that he was adamant he would never move to the bar. He was here first. Almost playfully he shuffled the few remaining pages, glanced at one, and was frankly amazed that there could have been such pain from it earlier. Katy had seemed so callous to him, so selfish and unfeeling. He had cursed her for her triviality, for making their love so trivial, and for her disloyalty. Now that he had come to the photograph, he could see that was all wrong. There was no evil in her, she was just pretty Kate, and he called up another picture of her, sitting naked in bed, imagined quite easily all the polished gradations of her perfect skin, her long hair the color of ambershot ale—

"Did you want something to eat?"

This was Donna. He reorganized himself to focus on her. "Sure," he said. "Great idea."

"But what? I will need more information, sir."

"A pizza?" said Doug, aware that she had said something funny in a good-natured way, yet unable to respond properly. "Plain cheese pizza?"

"Sure. It'll be about fifteen minutes."

"I'll wait here," he said, trying to get himself back into the flow of their routine. He watched her walk toward the kitchen and wondered why her legs, in green tights, reminded him of potatoes. He wished the legs were perfect, with long smooth perfect muscles, like Katy's. He wished that Donna were just slightly beautiful and he thought, poor Donna, poor legs, and felt terribly sorry for her until somehow he recalled that Donna seemed perfectly cheerful.

Meanwhile he had skipped ahead to yesterday's letter, the most recent, like an impatient reader peeking at the ending.

Dear Doug,

Your farflung correspondent, on assignment in The Big Apple, where at last the World Series talk is fading away. It's bad enough that no one in New York believes any other place in the world truly exists, they also can't seem to believe any activity proceeds, other than baseball.

Mini-breakthrough to report. My immediate boss, this guy

Bill Kingman, liked some of my stuff well enough to carry it "upstairs" to Simonson. Just a start, but wouldn't it be amazing if if if if (say the brown bells of Cardiff)? And yes I know I am just being a goose, but the one he liked best was that fiction piece *you* liked, about the guy with the dogs. They don't use fiction, but what the hey, let 'em know what you can do, right?

But there's something else I need to talk about here—I guess I'm nervous to start. You know I have had a friendly "date" or two, coffee or a beer or what have you, and maybe you have done the same, why not? Bill asked me to go skiing with him in Vermont and that sort of thing I have *not* done. But I did sort of discover that I like feeling slightly unattached. Or maybe what I like is the illusion of feeling unattached when the protection of our attachment is there to fall back on. Very possibly so.

There are so many moments when I just miss you and can't believe we are where we are, and there are other times when I realize it's being "where we are"—you there, me here—that gives me my little bit of trite, trivial, silly "freedom."

Being honest, I should also say that I have gotten close to one particular guy here, a friend of Mary's who does camera work for several different publications. But he is not trying to monopolize me at all. On the contrary, he is downright doctrinaire about people staying open, and free, so you can believe it is nothing serious, Doug. Roger is just one of the thousands of interesting people in this city—one I happened to meet.

No final Thanksgiving plan yet, but I will be home Thur and Fri at the very least, so we will have a chance to talk all this over if you want.

Love,
Kate

Doug doubled the rubber band around his sheaf of letters and let it snap. He fed cold pizza slices to his face, staring at the funhouse reflection of himself in the mug. These passages had seared him earlier, almost disgusted him with their casual revelations, their insincerities and evasions, murkiest of transitions. But it was all one big murky transition, wasn't it, over the absurdly short course of seven weeks, from a time when she allegedly dreamt of him every night, to the present, when she and Roger Photographer were nothing serious.

Hell of a transition, to be sure, but somehow the words and even what lay behind them did not upset him now. At the moment, he was full of good fellowship—happy for Bill Skiwax, happy for Roger Photographer, concerned about Donna . . . Or was Donna just one of the thousands of interesting people in Braxton, no more and no less? Doug doubted that Roger P. had lumpy potato legs, though, Rog would have lean legs, designer jean legs, and look like Christopher Reeve or a tall Tom Cruise, with lots of teeth.

It was past eight on the Genessee 12-Horse Clock above the row of flashing bottles, and with ale up to his eyelids, Doug was definitely ready for a change of air, a look at the Braxton County harvest moon. He gained his feet on the second launch and stood wrestling with the question of a tip—would a very large tip be insulting in some obscure way?—when Donna appeared.

"Goodnight," she said.

"It's been a pleasure—thanks to you. Thank you."

"Drive carefully on your way home."

"I'm walking," he said, though this was not the case. "But I will walk carefully."

"You never did end up asking me out."

"I didn't? It's hard to remember what I asked. Anyway, I lied," he lied. "I *am* a writer. So you see—"

"I thought you were. I was trying to decide if I'd make an exception for you. In my rule."

"That's awfully nice of you, even to think of it. But I've got kids, I'm afraid—you know, a wife and kids. Got to get home now. So thanks again, really."

"You do not."

"I do, I do," he said, by now openly fleeing toward the shining street and the high chill shimmering moon. He had a sudden infusion of terror about Donna, nothing to do with legs or that, it just seemed she held the power to bring him down, like an anchor; this wondrous new equanimity somehow depended on his staying alone with the letters.

He was fine, he was solid, afloat—solidly floating toward his car—but it was very tenuous. He did not want to see the wrong sights, or invite the wrong images in. The evening was brassy and right, full of fine autumn swirl, and the call of his own warm bed back home was sufficient, even delicious in prospect. Kate was beautiful, the world was surely beautiful—*life* was, dammit—and sliding under the steering wheel Doug realized he was still grinning like a fool. Hours. And right then he was hit with one huge heavy shot to the heart, a slab of iron wedged under his breastbone, that flashed an unmistakable message of distress and oblivion to all his organs, but he sat, and breathed, and let it pass.

The engine rasped and caught, and Doug wasted no time, leaping through the carcluttered intersection like a salmon splashing up against the violent white water, loud happy music booming in his ears.

Domestic Tranquility

It began with a nasty screaming bout one Sunday morning when their son was at a friend's house. Neither of them could recall anymore what had inspired it, and of course it would never have happened at all had Robert been at home.

But the screaming had grown worse in the car—much worse—and it was there that Karen lost it altogether. Literally foaming at the mouth, she started sweeping objects off the dashboard, whipping them out the window. A tin of Band-aids, the old chipped scraper, map fragments—flinging them backhand one after another and shrieking until finally, inevitably, she pitched George's 4-way screwdriver.

This was the only tool he owned, really, at any rate the only one he ever used; if the screwdriver couldn't get it done, then George couldn't either. It had been weathering agreeably on the dash for years. When he saw it go, George stopped the car, backed up, and spent the next twenty minutes sifting through the roadside brush. The brush yielded plenty of treasure—bottles and cans and faded paper—but it did not yield up the 4-way. It was impossible to prolong the search with Robert waiting for them, and really it seemed hopeless anyhow. At least Karen had quieted down.

It festered, however. George feigned good nature for the boy, naturally, and went about a Sunday's business of clawing his way through the newspaper, tending the yard. They even had a drink that afternoon with the Carlsons next door and though George was far from scintillating, he was certainly pleasant. Karen herself would never have guessed how it was festering.

It wasn't just the loss of the 4-way, it was the stupidity and malice in her action. If George "needed" to kick a wall, he would still take care not to break his own toe, or seriously damage the plaster. Surely one could express anger, even rage, without suffering total blackout. That was for psychopaths—the ones who could appear so clean-cut and normal in court yet in a wild rage had taken six lives some icy night last February.

Even so, George was surprised to awaken in the same dark state of mind on Monday. Again he passed, rushing off to work, but clearly there had been no real emotional resolution. Something as trivial as this spat should simply dissolve into the morass of their lives and for Karen it had—whoosh and gone for her, always, like the screwdriver—she'd left it all behind at the scene of the crime. And hers was without question the healthier response; he dared not even broach a displeasure which it was incorrect to harbor still and whose disbursement, moreover, just might start her screaming again.

The solution came to him at his desk, a sure way to dissipate this cold unwelcome fury. An eye for an eye, someone at the office had said in some regard, a tossed-off saw of the sort no one even hears: but why *not* an eye? Why not rough justice? Karen had a particular wire whisk in her kitchen that was irreplaceable in the exact same way the 4-way was, namely that there were other whisks in the world but this one was hers, it pleased her out of habit and familiarity. The ones she could buy were somehow minutely different, were at the very least different whisks. Where the punishment so precisely fit the crime, could there not be justice for all? And without a lot of hubbub.

Late that night he slid the whisk into his briefcase; next day, downtown, slid it out and flipped it into a blue dumpster with a most gratifying clangor. He knew he was partaking of the selfsame foolishness and waste he deplored in her action, and he also knew some shame. Karen had been malicious in broad daylight, as it were. The daylight here was broad enough, but George was skulking nonetheless. Shouldn't he be doing this to her face, *in* her face, both in fairness and for full impact?

Well, no, this was best. The grudge he harbored was "wrong" and the point therefore was not to dramatize but rather to discharge it, to work through it without making matters any worse. And the pragmatic approach did seem to pan out: by the time he came home the air was clear, the smile he had for Karen was real, the roast she had cooked for him was delicious, and it seemed the dust of that roadside lunacy had truly settled. Their life together could resume as dull and cheerful as ever.

George didn't mind dull. He accepted and even liked it (as he saw it, a pleasant orderly life would *have* to be a little dull) and moving toward the weekend and a cookout with the Carlsons, he was positively radiant with resolution. Friday night, however, he couldn't find *Barrett's Chess Gambits* in its customary niche on the mantel and was about to hassle Robert for moving it when the truth belatedly struck home—Karen. She had figured out about the whisk and this was her return salvo. She had taken his favorite chess book and burned it, or wrapped up last night's bluefish in its hallowed pages. The battle was joined.

For George, guerilla warfare had its delights and its nasty surprises; on the whole it suited. He particularly liked the quiet of it, and the creative latitude it gave him to strike as he chose and when he chose. Indeed, he waited fully a week before flushing her grandmother's moth-eaten silk hankie down the toilet. The hideous rag was worthless, of course, yet in selecting it George felt he had met all the requirements of the contest, of which (to his way of thinking) there were three. The choice must punish, clearly, and it must also be slightly—yet only slightly—malicious. And thirdly, the condition most easily met, virtually an automatic, it should entail idiotic wastefulness. Karen had set these standards and if there was to be edification for her, the standards would have to be upheld.

And so they were. There never came an escalation; this remained a small war, a ground war fought with conventional weapons in purely guerilla fashion. No peace talks commenced because no declaration of hostilities had ever been made or even vaguely acknowledged. Neither of them once alluded to any missing item, so neither indulged a visible emotion over any loss, though each object was held dear and beyond all value. The understanding, the contract, was so complete that Robert had no sense of roaming freely in the militarized zone; the boy felt perfectly safe.

There were aspects that began to bother George as the weeks went by. Now the battle lines were drawn, for one, wherein lay victory? Or failing victory, resolution? In the beginning, victory had not been a goal; Karen had erred and George had sought to adjudicate, or at least offset, the error. Yet from her first retaliation *(Barrett's Chess Gambits)* Karen had shown a disinclination to truck with Justice. It was as though she did not agree she was wrong about the screwdriver (not even after quiet reflection!) and therefore incurred no retribution. It was this terrible, untenable position that had made the game into something more and more like war, cruel and partisan.

This too bothered George, for at the outset there had been an agreeable lightness, a humorous edge to the proceedings, as though they were having *fun,* almost. *It* was not dull. Now the fun had gone from it and a distinct grimness had settled on them in its stead. The awful screaming, he realized, had silently lasted, for months.

Larger questions arose. Should it end, could it end, and if not what did it mean? Must they enlist in joint therapy? Would they need to divorce? What *was* this? Most women who were murdered, George read, were done in by their husbands; was this how that came about?

One night, trailing 5–4 on the scoreboard, he finally imagined an ending to the awful impasse. He would counter the loss of his old fraternity lavaliere by deepsixing Karen's desk calendar sometime in the next day or two. Then, with the score knotted at 5–5, and before anything else could happen, he would open the discussion he'd had a hundred times in his mind.

"Isn't this getting pretty stupid?" he would say. Or: "Aren't we both being awfully stubborn?" But say it with affection somehow, say it without a trace of vindictiveness.

Unfortunately, he knew—*knew*—what she would say in

reply: "You started it." He would need a good response to that—something vague and nonpartisan, if possible something affectionate—most definitely something other than, "No, *you* started it." The fact that he could imagine no conclusion to the dialogue had helped to keep it, thus far, from beginning; but they would just have to play it by ear. Christ, maybe it would even end in wonderful heedless laughter and sex, the way their fights always used to end.

But first must come the tying heist. The desk calendar was a good choice (Karen was so totally dependent on those scribble-filled pages that he almost hated to do it) and perhaps it was the excitement that kept George awake, then vexed his threadbare sleep with dreams. He dreamt he was creeping toward her desk when the room suddenly exploded with light and there she stood, fierce and resolute in rippling bandoleros studded with bright silver bullets.

Too shaky to act in the morning, George went to work but came home early with a touch of late summer flu. Karen brought a pot of tea and sat on the bed with him watching the news. The Red Sox lost by a run in the ninth. "Another tough loss," he groaned, and Karen consoled him: "Maybe it should be like tennis. You know— where you have to win by two?"

She smiled and went back downstairs and George knew he would never get a shot at the calendar. He knew in his heart she had changed the rules, was in the den right now rummaging among his topographical survey maps. It was not her turn, but he knew she was going anyway, going out of turn. Win by two.

He didn't even care; had no more stomach for trouble; knew for certain that defeat would be far less serious in fact than it was in prospect. It was over, or it would be, and as soon as he shook off this germ their lives could return to normal, to the *status quo ante bellum*. That was how it was with wars, they never changed a damn thing but they could kill you just the same.

The Golden Gate Funeral March

Ma might have said it as a joke, just to give us all something to laugh over and herself to relax a bit, she might
have never meant a thing by it. But then again she might
have, and I wasn't taking any chances: if it was her wish
to go to the Golden Gate Bridge, then that's exactly where
we would take her. It's a long way of course, and the Boss
had already come a long way (up from Bluefield last week)
but we figured just do it, so we did. Got packed, set Ma
up in the back seat as tender as possible under the circumstances, and simply wung it out across the Thruway to
Buffalo and Points West.

Did I say we're starting out from Schenectady? That's
where Ma has been living, just the other side of Schenectady in Cohoes. I keep a room in Duanesburg, mainly
because with both Pa and the Boss gone south, someone
had to stay close by. Anyway I took Pa's job with the
turnpike when he went off, and Duanesburg's as good as
any in that respect. I wouldn't want to be right in the city,
like when we first came up. I was fourteen then and we
all came up because there was supposed to be jobs in Troy
and there wasn't, but in Schenectady Pa got taken at the
turnpike authority.

Troy, Greece, Rome, Utica, Ithaca. They got all those,
which I believe come from an ancient myth, and then

they got the Indian ones, which I personally like, such as
Cheektowaga and Irondequoit, and Seneca. Buffalo and
Niagara too, I guess, though I prefer the ones you get less
often—Tonawanda and Oneonta and so on. When we first
got north Pa told me they were actually all reservations
(with the real Indians in their wigwams drinking liquor)
and I did believe it, as I was a kid. But Pa may have
believed it too, as he was no special wizard and someone
may have just told it to him for truth. Of course in time
we saw some of those towns and saw they were like any
other, with your stores and gas-ups and mainstreet lunch-
rooms.

Anyhow we blew out to Buffalo like nothing that first
day with Ma, did it in under five hours and kept right on
going to the Points West, though it was rough and cold
along that Lake Erie with no heater in the Boss' Chevy.
We were shooting for Cleveland, maybe even Chicago if
we stuck to plan, but Boss was tired and we both were
turning blue in the breeze, this being November.

"You know something, Jerry?" he said. "We are right
this minute closer to Bluefield than we are to Schenectady.
That is right."

"Don't feel right," I said, meaning how cold it was.

"But doesn't this start to feel stupid?"

"Can't argue with Ma."

"No, but I can see doing it different. Why not take
her home? Head south right now—or in the morning,
whatever."

"To Bluefield instead?"

"Sure."

"Boss, come on. We been pushing it too hard, that's
all. Let's find some coffee and some food. This one's my
treat."

"I'm for that."

That didn't mean he changed his mind. He'd be for it no matter, just as a pit stop. But I know Boss, he wouldn't change his mind. All the way west he'd be convinced we were doing this wrong, all the way west he'd talk about turning back. That was just how he had sized it up. Yet by the same token he would never act on it, he'd keep on all the way to Golden Gate cause that was the plan and that was what we had to do.

We came into one of those HoJo's where they sell you a two-dollar hot dog and they did have you because you'd go five for the hot dog and another two for coffee at that point. Boss headed straight inside while I hung a moment not knowing what to do with Ma. Leave her in the back seat seemed easiest, yet it felt bad to me. I did it that way, though, reasoning if we brought her inside all kinds of accidents could happen. She was safest, at least, in the back seat.

Boss was settled in there, sprawled like a drunken lord in fact, burning up a Lucky and already sipping hot coffee. Coming at him across the room I saw him almost as a stranger, especially with his big new moustaches. But definitely he had aged. I hadn't lived with him like a brother in nearly twenty years yet here was the first moment in all that time I felt apart from him. First time I took stock it *was* twenty years, for God's sake. When the years was so *like* one another (not to mention the days and the hours), time could gain on you far too easy. And this all led by the time I sat down to a snap idea—quit the turnpike authority and get something new going.

I meditated on this as we ate, the hot dogs and beans with brown bread they have, and except for how nice and warm it was (and how good food could taste, etcetera) we hadn't a lot to say to each other until it was time to put off from port. Boss was picking at his teeth with a jack-knife, which is a nasty habit he's got, though not half so nasty as when he goes one better. If he comes up against a tough one, like say corn, or steak, you know, he will just take the teeth out and work on them right there on his placemat, casual as a factory girl. So this with the jackknife was not so bad. I think he believed it was a part of his well-being, cause at one time he informed me all the rich men picked their teeth at dinner. I didn't and don't know what to make of that and though I did once ask him why it was the case, the Boss answered it was merely an observation, such as the one that dogs will chase cats. He couldn't tell you *why* dogs will chase cats, and yet he had seen it often enough to know it for a fact.

I don't see that much of Boss these days. He went back to Bluefield after the Army and except for coming up to help with Ma he only comes north once a year, at Christmas. Likewise I go down once a year. I always take my vacation in the middle of March and I see him there. Always loved the look of it that time of year, never forgot any of it. I might have gone back myself if not for Ma and my spot at the authority.

"So will you stay west?" I asked him, opening up a subject partly just to dodge the cold. But I also was thinking, as I mentioned, about quitting my job.

"I doubt."

"Me neither. But where?"

"What do you mean? Where's easy. Right back home. This is just an automobile ride to me, Jerry—I wasn't thinking about the west coast before Ma insisted and I'm not thinking about it now. Just taking her where she wants to be."

"You really like it so much still?"

"I know all the shortcuts."

"There's that. But with Ma gone, we'll have to think of something, won't we? I mean, hell, Boss, you're forty-one."

"Don't remind me." He grinned when he said that and picked between the front teeth.

"Well it is true."

"All the more reason."

"I've been thinking of marriage," I said, maybe surprising myself more than I surprised the Boss.

"Oh yes? Congratulations, boy. Is the lucky individual anyone I know?"

"She isn't even anyone I know, yet. I'm talking about as a thing to do, something I would like to try."

"More power," said Boss. He could get to me with his complacent ideas about life. To him it was all the same.

"I mean without mentioning *your* age at all, I'll turn thirty-five myself next month. And don't say happy birthday either, you dull son of a bitch."

"What the hell is eating at you, boy?"

"Nothing is. It's just you never mean anything, you never think a thing through. You ignore it all, and I don't want to be that kind of ignorant."

"More power," goes the Boss.

"You dumb shit, there you go again. It's no better than a burp when you talk."

I can't say why, because I had always looked up to Boss, him being six years my older brother and all, and I never gave him such lip as this. Never thought such thoughts, to be truthful, but even if I had I would sooner bite my tongue, as the Boss had generally cuffed me around pretty good and I had come to recognize a twinge of fear when

he got that look on him. The serpent look. So I don't
know why but this time I felt so different, felt in fact like
pitching a sharp rock at his dull-assed face. And he must
have known it too because he did not rise to the bait one
inch. Which was unlike him. He said nothing in reply
to me, though he made himself belch and then grinned
stupidly.

"You're one hell of a waste of time," I said, getting up.
"I'm going out to check on Ma."

I pitched a ten-dollar bill onto the table to cover costs
and had turned to leave when the dumb fuck suddenly
began to laugh hysterically. I tried to glare him but he
smiled me down.

"Just reminded me," he said, snickering away. "The
other night, at the package store, when you were waiting
in the car? Well this little China man comes in cackling
like a hen, all excited, and he flips a ten down on the
counter, just like you did? Cuts in front of me, lays down
his money, and says, Shits ten dolla shits ten dolla."

"What?"

"Right. What. The salesman looks at him, hasn't got a
clue, so the China guy does it some more, like a goddam
parrot with just these words to his name. Shits ten dolla,
shits ten dolla. Me and the salesman just shrug at each
other, you know. Does this guy need to use the head and
think it costs ten bucks? Then it hits us, both at the same
second. The little dude wants to buy a case of Schlitz,
that's the special of the week. Schlitz ten dollars, is what
he's been saying. And sure enough, that's it, that's what
he wants. Gets his brew and goes off gay as a bird."

I was forced to ease off him by all this storytelling but
left him there smoking and grinning so I could get outside
to Ma. The Boss didn't care about Ma anymore, I guess,

this was just another chore she laid on him, where to me of course it was sad as hell, there was this pain in my chest if I even looked at her. I'd been checking on her often, even knowing she'd be no better no worse. I did want to see her without Boss in the car so I could talk to her without being labeled a retard, but he came right behind my heels and put us back in gear, to the Points West.

We kept going all night as it turned out, stopping at the side of the road for a catnap and then not stopping again till we hit a breakfast someplace southwest of Chicago. I had never seen the country before and I wasn't seeing it now. We had crossed nearly half of it, and turnpike and darkness was all it was for me. What I mainly craved was sleep, while he kept summarizing all the dollars we saved by not sleeping. He was into the trip on a theory level now, seeing how cheap we could travel crosscountry. Announced he would be putting out a new bestseller, America on Ten Dollars a Day or what-have-you. He was in high spirits, Boss was, for a dullard who hadn't slept in two days, and I bought the breakfast to show we had no hard feelings, though maybe we had.

"It'll help with your book."

"How's that?"

"America on ten dollars a day. The secret is take along your brother and he pays twenty dollars a day. Get it?"

"Got it."

The hard feelings I had were not his fault, I realized, and that's why I kept them to myself. It was this: in the back of my mind I always figured Boss and I would someday have a business together. That was why I wished he would shape himself up and talk serious about things and that was why I was playing out the idea of quitting the turnpike. I wanted to be partners in a business and I always expected he would be the one with the idea for it, the inspiration. I had all this time been waiting to hear from him on the subject and somehow it was just dawning on me I would never hear a word, it was the farthest from his mind, such as it was. That's what got me mad—Boss didn't care what he did and he didn't care about me.

When we were parked back there to catch a few winks (which he managed and I never came close) I watched him, took a really good look at him. My brother, my hero, yet the son of a gun was one ungainly slob. Head thrown back in a snore, mouth hung open, and his damn teeth in the change tray on the dash, in among the dimes and quarters. Let him rot, I was thinking, he is not my hero one inch. He was, though, and it made me want to fling his damn teeth into a Great Lake.

Of course I didn't, I let be his plate, for you see we were all business in this one respect, get it *done,* and so we horsed all day into that cold snowylooking turnpike air. We were worn and saying little, just drove and drove, clear across the state of Iowa into the state of Nebraska, these being a few of the Points West they had promised us back in Buff City. So there was just this strange matter of moving damn fast while sitting perfectly still, except for the one highlight of the day, North Platte.

Nebraska is mostly flat and empty and the Boss says in the warm months it smells like shit (meaning of course the fertilizer) and North Platte is not too different apart from its historic significance as the spot where our Uncle Edgar, Ma's kid brother and her favorite, was kissed by a truck. Ma always used to say Edgar might have been kissed on the sly by some cousin truck years earlier because he had this crooked face, almost like a pervert in the old family pictures. Neither of us saw North Platte coming, didn't even register we would be going through it, yet it clicked right away when the first sign appeared, for this was one of the colorful stories often told.

Edgar was a motorcycle man, kept a whole fleet apparently of the old Indian bikes, if you ever saw one, and this all happened back in the Thirties. At that time some of the big Pierce-Arrow hauling rigs had carbon lamps on the side, not out front where the electric headlights would be, and so naturally these lamps sit far apart, one on each side of the rig. At night, or in the twilight, it might look as though two bikers were coming down the road side by side, instead of a truck at all. Now Edgar was a notorious lover of fun, and drink I guess, and as the story goes he saw those lights coming at him and being naturally half off the wall at all times took a notion to really sail down that strip and cleave right between the two bikes. That is how the story goes.

They did pull him out of the radiator, though, that much is sure. And I imagine he might have had quite a moment there when he was set to sail on through with a whoop and then suddenly saw the hood ornament and all that steel behind it. Lord. That's North Platte. And Ma used to ride with him sometimes.

It isn't funny and it is, but we were laughing until I thought of Ma in the back seat. Maybe we were so frozen cold and punchy that anything could get us started. We were going for Cheyenne, Wyoming by night and we would make it too, the way Boss turned up his nose at each and every sleepy hollow we passed. This one too big and that one too small, too close to the highway—too *gaudy* even was one of them! I guess he was trying to slice it down to five dollars. Finally there came a perfect one, halfway back up a smooth little hill, nice cabins, and free morning coffee advertised. The billboard, though, said they had Military Government Rates, which got the Boss rolling once again.

"Jer, we ain't *in* the Military Government."

This time I was prepared to be firm. Forty straight hours out of Cohoes by here. "There *ain't* no Military Government in this country, it's just a sign. It doesn't say they don't have normal rates too."

"I know it, one arm and one leg."

"I'll treat," I said per usual, and he relented to try. We took it and what a grand idea to do so, because this place was warm and the beds there were big and soft even for a civilian like ourselves. I brought Ma in from the cold and just fell out for twelve hours solid of wall-to-wall sleeping and sweet dreaming. Must have done a hundred or so little dreams that night, all of them fine. Dreamed of Uncle Edgar on his old Indian except in the dream he didn't hit. He was about to, but right before the smash his bike sailed up and flew overtop the rig. And kept on flying over the road and the trees toward the sunset, which had a big sign on it saying Golden Gate and Points West.

Sleep was a grand idea that changed everything for the better. I woke up happy, Ma's condition notwithstanding, and the day was bright, and it seemed all a man could need just to shower and shave and drink his morning coffee. The Boss was a grade sharper himself, even insisted on splitting the cost right down the middle. You see, now we had it made. Downhill side, as the Boss put it, meaning here we are in goddam Wyoming on a clear golden morn and at the very least we are going to *make* it to the coast.

Two things I can recommend without reserve in the state of Wyoming. One is the scenery. What an all-out beautiful place they have got themselves, ranches and rolling hills, big shade trees, miles of handmade fence with horses, and then the mountains too. My second recommend is in a spot called Raving Gorge or something along those lines, it's the Raving Gorge Donut Hole I believe, where for one dollar we got thirteen of the finest treats I ever tasted. I did three honeydipped right there in the Rising Gorge lot and three chocolate frosted the next forty miles, still not even to Utah yet.

"Bossman," I said, "you gonna want all six of yours?" I forgot the baker's dozen and thought I'd used up my own.

"I don't want any of them."

"Are you kidding? These are choice morsels. Besides which, it's breakfast." I was talking him toward the doughnuts while simultaneously hoping him past them.

"I don't eat that crap," said Boss. "Just let me have a little more of the coffee in a minute."

"You got it," I said, and went on to the lemon dream and the raspberry cream, then rested a bit before taking on the first of the apple crunch. Boss was in a good mood, he just really did not care for doughnuts. These ones were special, though, and kept me nibbling away till there was only powdered left in the box. I don't care for powdered but had just tasted one and not minded it when we heard the siren go and saw a mountie on our necks. This was the town of Murdo, which state I can't recall. The rest I do recall.

Mountie pulled us over at the ramp and then sat in his cruiser a few minutes picking nose. When he finally came up and pushed his bully puss on us, Boss handed him the papers and asked what was the problem. Cause it sure wasn't us.

"Got you coming down that hill half a mile back, got you at ninety miles per hour."

"You are reaching there, officer," said the Boss, in his

friendly voice. "This vehicle can do nothing close to the ninety mile figure you stated."

The funny thing about my brother is nothing much ever did scare him. Being scared is about as foreign to him as being smart is. He's just a dull thud all around. Which comes handy in a situation where there are mounties and one of you *is* scared, properly.

"Got it on the gun," said the law. "You boys will have to follow me to town."

"Town, hell," said the Boss. "Where's the ticket? Hadn't you better write up your phony ticket?"

"Son, you are looking at a speeding charge here but if you keep giving me face I'm going to have to add to those charges heavily."

I managed to get us rolling, into the town of Murdo, which was of the one-horse western variety, a little dust-bunny blown down off the interstate. Our man swung us through the filling station there to speak a word with the chief of grease, who then accompanied us across the main drag to a square brick box labelled Town of Murdo on the lintel. It was one room inside—a desk and two benches, some dusty files, a moonfaced clock up on the wall like school days, plus a potbelly stove the mountie stoked up with a clutch of kindling.

"Mr. Farley here is our Justice of the Peace," he said, and Mr. Farley came forth minus his wrench now, bald and smiling, and gave us a nice greasy handshake. "Mr. Farley, these boys were up to ninety miles per hour on the Jackson Hill."

"Bull shit, Mr. Farley," said the Boss. "You take my Chevy over to your garage there and tune it up good and tight. Get it all hummy, smooth as a goose, and then go out and hit seventy-five in it if you can."

"Now Mr. Farley is not here in a mechanic or testdriving capacity, son. He's J.P. in this town, fully empowered to accept your waiver of trial."

"Let's have trial," said the Boss.

"Fair enough, fair enough. The only problem is our circuit judge won't be by for another two weeks. Thursday the seventeenth will find him here in Murdo. And I would have to hold you until that date."

"I get it," said Boss. He looked explosive to me.

"What happens," I said, "if we waive trial?" I caught my reward in an evil eye from the Boss that could shatter plexiglas.

"Nothing much. You plead to it, we fine you, and you go."

"How much?"

"The fine? Well, let me look that up—here, it'd be one hundred dollars as a first offense, which this is. So one hundred dollars."

"We don't have it," I said, though we did have it. We needed all we had, of course, and had the bulk of it well stashed. "Suppose we waive trial and send you the cash when we get where we're going?"

"No, that doesn't work out. How much *do* you have?"

"Maybe twenty-five."

"Not too close."

"I can write you a check."

"That doesn't work out. Maybe if we look over your vehicle and see what you have, it's always possible the circumstances can be extenuated a bit to accommodize you."

At that the Boss spit one and it nearly landed on the filthy crook's boot. I thought it a fearful bad idea, yet had to like it all the same. Boss was shaking off the extenuation:

"We ain't no monkey men, you know," was what he said. Which meant exactly nothing to the mountie and the chief of grease, nevertheless constituting a major big deal to my brother. He has always had this thing where he imagines a whole tribe of little spidery guys with round eyes and stubby noses—he got this from someone in the service, I believe—and they supposedly have distant invisible Negro blood in them but are never a hit with the ladies. The Boss is missing second gear no question, maybe reverse as well, but he can get very upset about this matter of the monkey men. Sees them on the street and gets all worked up, sees them getting into politics. He had me worried I was one, back when I was seventeen and small and certainly no hit with the ladies myself. And Boss was certain beyond a reasonable doubt that Pa was one. Pa being a monkey man explained it all to Boss, put all the pieces in place, though I told him Pa couldn't be one if he had got Ma, if you see what I mean.

"Whatever you say, pal," said the law now, declining to rule on the monkey man issue. "But you must pay your fine or else stand trial. That's the statute."

"I thought," said I, "we were innocent till proven guilty."

"You were. I mean you are. But if you sign a confession, you see, then that's otherwise."

Boss spit another one and I felt nervous as a cat in the corner. And then the Justice of Peace began to step into his role a bit—we later figured they had it all scripted out ahead of time—and he come in on our side, more or less.

"Can't squeeze blood from a stone, though, Ray," he said to the mountie, who stood meanlooking and wordless behind those standard-fare wraparound shades with the one-way glare glass. Made him look like a mean windshield, was what.

"The thing to do, Raymundo, is this: see what they got in stock, see what can be worked out."

Back to the extenuation, in other words. The chief had to have his costume too in their little drama so he slipped into some gold-rimmed granny glasses, to highlight his sweet and intellectual side. And he did look kindly to me at the time, in his greasy overalls and quiet voice. In his kindly way he rifled our pockets and then somehow the whole tea party shifted out front to where the Chevy and the cruiser sat parked. There, still softly and also restraining the mountie from touching anything himself, the greaser of the peace ran through the trunk, inside-outed the duffels, surveyed the contents of the glove slot. I wasn't worried about our cash, which was mostly tucked up inside the busted radio speaker, but then the greaser spotted Ma in the back seat.

"What's that?"

"You leave that alone," Boss warned him. I was out of it for a second then, just couldn't think what to do at all, but Boss came through. Came right to life, as needed.

"Look in there," said the mountie to his partner in crime.

"Keep your greasy paws off that."

"What the hell is it, boys?" said Mr. Farley, most courteous still, our friend in court.

"It's our Ma," I told him, figuring the truth had to come out and (since it wasn't anything against the law) telling might get them to show some respect.

"Oh sure," said the mountie, "and this here is my sister's second cousin." He took out a pack of cheroots to make his little joke.

"It is her. We're carrying her west to scatter her ashes, in accord with her final wishes. The box looks fancy but it just comes free from the place that cremates."

"You serious?"

"Yes sir. We're taking her to San Francisco, to toss her off the Golden Gate Bridge."

"You can't do a crazy thing like that."

"It's for sure we can," said Boss.

"It's legal," went I.

"It's crazy," went the J.P., "but it probably is legal, Ray."

"It's eyewash. How do we know that box isn't full of money? Or goddamned narcotics for that matter."

He reached in for Ma's container and Boss just touched him. "I wouldn't. I told you, we ain't no monkey men."

"You said that before. I'm not expecting to find bananas in there if that's what you're thinking." He started again and this time I had a crack at it.

"Sir, you can understand that we don't care to see anyone but ourselves holding our mother's remains. That's all my brother means to say."

"That's understandable enough, boys," said Mr. Farley. "Why don't *you* open her up for us then—"

"I'm the fuckin sheriff here!" said the other though, all fired up suddenly, and before we could interfere again he darted in and grabbed Ma. Boss was loath to unload on him since now he held her. So he had us froze. And then opened it. I was churning away inside.

"Just ashes, Ray," said Mr. Farley.

"Might be something tucked in among them, Mr. Farley," said the law and before I could think the bastard had dumped Ma out on the street, right there in the gutter. I went blind. I dozed him over backwards and kicked his head, and I kept kicking him till they dragged me off, the Boss and Mr. Farley, then broke loose and started sweeping together Ma's bits and pieces with my bare hands. I was blind mad and blurry crying the whole while but this had to be done and done quick, for even in the soft wind some of her fluttered up and some more was smeared black on the cold paving.

Boss held open the box and talked to me, saying stuff, but I just couldn't handle the idea of her being upset like that, with some part of her gone into the middle of Nowhere Utah, forever gone, though the Boss kept telling me we had her all, we had her all. I suppose we had ninety percent of her but the missing ten was to me a cruel piece, and always would be. I knew that then.

Mr. Farley was all sweet reason still, and told us to give over the cash we had plus my wristwatch and get on route before the sheriff came back to the mark. "It's best all around," he said. "You lost your temper—maybe you had good cause, I see that. But Ray Gillis won't see that and he wears the badge. You get out and leave the money, I'll talk him around the fine points. I'll buy him a nice bottle down the street and talk him around it. Be fine if you just hustle now."

"Fuck him and his nice bottle," said my brother, and pushed his boot down on the mountie's neck. But we went along with it, gave the watch and the cash, which Mr. Farley pronounced shy but adequate at $28, and took the highway with one hellish bad feeling in the gut. Ma on the street back there, and our money, and that pig-knuckle shit of a sheriff . . . The road ahead looked dark and cold again.

We were torn between racing away and crawling, for no doubt another crooked officer of the law lay crouched behind certain future billboards and brush piles. Then too, it was late. Might have set our hats for Reno as the next town of size, except it was too far to go for the way we were feeling, and the weather played a factor as well. Day was done. We pulled in to a truck stop offering good food and layover cots, and sat down in the half that was for the general public, sat up at the counter. Boss always felt it was somehow cheaper when you sat at the counter, though of course it wasn't.

I ordered cheeseburgers well done and pie with coffee, Boss took the blue plate special of shepherd's pie with succotash on the side, and we said our usual nothing until the food was dispatched and the Boss was smoking.

"Jerry, you trashed your first sheriff."

"Guess I did."

"Done like a true blue honkytonk hippie."

"Done like a crazy man, if that's what you mean." I was shaking my head, for never in my life before had I acted that way or even close to it.

"You did look over the edge, boy. Your whole head looked so damn tight, like it'd just been pulled through a knothole or something."

"Can't say I'm sorry, with what he did."

"Hell no. *Sorry?*"

"No."

"Was a good day up to then, Jer. But those mountains? Man, if you'd been paying attention you'd a been scared shitless on some of those roads."

"I was paying attention."

"To your doughnuts," he laughed. I laughed with him, but I had seen him doing his donkey dance on those skinny passes, hanging out over the loose shoulder, and wooden crosses all along the ditch. I just stayed quiet so he wouldn't be hassled while he drove it.

"You drove like a pro, Boss. After Murdo, too."

"After fuckin Murdo, boy, I was *gone,* like a ruptured duck in a hailstorm. If we stayed a minute longer, or left a minute slower, we would have killed that fuckin mountie."

I couldn't disagree. My emotions were bad while the Boss seemed free and easy, but fine by me to be agreeing on everything for a precious few minutes. I knew it wouldn't last long. We were bent on banging heads this trip and soon enough we got it going over some old hen from Seattle, Washington. She had been there at the counter with us and at some point in the proceedings started in telling us her life. Actually it was everybody's life *but* hers, friends and relatives and even people she had only heard about; they all fell in one basket to her and the basket was hospitals and doctors.

She was old and I guess worried about dying, so all she could think about was setbacks and seizures. It was one terrible operation after another, her whole world was keeling over, and she did take us on one hell of a depressing tour of every hospital in the west. Worse part was she had a real flair for the gory, piling on lots of phlegm and blood. But she was only being friendly in her own peculiar way and, as I told Boss later on, she was somebody's Ma herself. You think about things that way and you end up acting better. But the Boss didn't think, he showed no class.

The poor biddie says to us finally, Oh dear I must be boring you boys to distraction, expecting we would say Oh no and all that, but instead Boss goes, "It is getting pretty bad, actually." And she tried to get out graceful then, said she was sorry, it was just she had been through a lot, and Boss goes, "So have we, lady, so have we"—

meaning her. He would not let her off, she just plain ran in the end. Fired out of there like a chicken with her wings clipped.

Boss thought it one grand joke but it put me off by myself again. I ate my pie (thinking, I confess, of the Flaming Gorge doughnuts instead) and said nothing to him until we were outside by the Chevy.

"I hope you're proud."

"Right proud, in general."

"You know what I mean."

"That sick old lady?"

"Yeah. That."

"Come on, Jer, give me a break. I never claimed I was Jesus Christ."

"Just a scared old lady and you probably finished her off. She probably crawled away and had a stroke and died."

"No way. People like that, who'll say anything to anybody? They don't care who listens."

Damned if he wasn't mostly right about it. I was leaning on him for some reason, I needed to and he knew I did, but with Boss when he wasn't mad it was awfully hard just to *make* him mad. Because he didn't care about much, you see. And so it might have blown by us if he hadn't gone and polished up that joke of his.

"That damn sheriff spoiled it, you know," he said. I did indeed know it, so I gave no answer. "My book, I mean."

"How's this?"

"My bestseller, the ten-dollar-a-day book. How can you do America on ten dollars a day if the law hits you up for twenty-odd at every little hick town along the line?"

"Is that what you think? Is that the height of your emotions when your mother's ashes are tossed out on the street?"

"Slow down, boy, it's just a little joke."

"The hell with your dull-assed zero-brained jokes, I can't use them just now."

"More power."

"You *are* a dull son of a bee, you and your goddamned monkey men."

"Whatever."

"Boss, there are critical parts missing under your hood."

"Whatever."

At that I swung on him, he had me so mad. I suppose I wanted him to swing first but he wouldn't, so I swung and somehow missed him. He stepped back and did his grin.

"You really want to slug, don't you?" he said.

I swung again and this time got a piece of his hard skull, enough to bruise a knuckle of mine. His face turned half mean—I truthfully believe most of the old meanness was gone out of the Boss by forty-one—and he set up to slug with me. Then he held up a second, put up his palm like he was calling time-out or somesuch, and removed his teeth. Took them out of his face, laid them gentle as could be up on the dashboard, and came back at me with that sickly gumbo grin of his. I was gone. I never could get past it, it always cracked me up, to see him filing that hideous business away like a jeweler handling his prize wares.

"What the hell," he said. "No sense throwing away good money."

"You mean you expected me to land on you."

"You might. One lick? Sure you might, before I crushed you."

"I'm leaving mine in," I said, but of course there was no anger anymore, this was joking both ways.

"You got no choice, yours are still attached."

"What the hell."

And so on. Once it was gone, I let it go. It was about nothing in the first place. We turned around and took cots for the night, at two bills per—for we saw no point in stretching our necks out at this juncture, maybe six seven hours from the big Pacific puddle—and straightaway we both lay down though I knew I wasn't going to sleep this night. Weary to the bone, but I was restless too, and it bothered me how it was with me and Boss. It seemed we ought at least be pulling together now, while seeing after Ma's final wishes, yet no way would it happen. We were too different.

There lay the Boss, per usual, snoring along like a chainsaw and his damn teeth right by his side like the holy word. My hero snoring. But you know, he still had it, I still felt it back there on the street in Murdo. That old hummy feel—someone was pushing on us and the Boss would push back harder. It was there. If I hadn't lost my own head, the Boss would have done some far more serious work on that mountie's sorry form, I know it.

But what kept me awake and tossing on the cot that night was not about Boss or any of the sloppy adventures we'd had. It was Ma, of course. Above and beyond the shock of her spilled and partly lost (which to this very day does somersaults in my head) there was the other, that here for sure was my last night with her. By tomorrow afternoon she'd be truly and completely gone from us. So this was my last chance to talk to her, really directly, to be with her, and it made me sadder than I can tell you. A big wide pain in the chest when I went out to fetch her.

The white moon lay back behind what looked like the only cloud in the sky, just enough cloud to hold it, and I was happy the night had turned gentle.

I did talk to her under that gentle sky. I'm not ashamed. I had things to tell her before she went. I'll be something, I told her, I will get married soon. I won't be anything special, but I will be something. That is a promise. And then thinking how this was the last made me think again and almost change and say, Why pitch her? Why not keep her? I remembered why: she wanted it, so we had to do it. Couldn't talk her around it at this point, so I gave it up. Brought her inside and tossed some more in the big dormitory, where a host of truckers was snoring and it was nearly sunup anyway.

And that's all really. The rest was nothing much. We drove ahead to Frisco, set up midspan on the old Golden Gate, and there we did do what we came so far to do. I could tell you it was awfully high and windy up there, which it was, or that the wind took Ma's ashes every which way but loose, which it did. We were guiding them down and brushing them off the bridge and off ourselves, and they flew and fluttered and scattered like the crazy leaves of autumn. In the end they were mostly down in the water where I guess she wanted to be, and I said I hoped she was happy and I cried. Not Boss. He just said he hoped seeing what happened to her on the bridge had made me feel better about what happened in Murdo to her. It did and it didn't, since this was by our hand and in accord with her wishes.

Yet nothing special occurred. We didn't get ourselves arrested on the bridge or knock out the national guards, or anything like that. And nothing special took place afterwards either. We had some brews and poked around Frisco

town but we never won the Irish Sweepstakes or anything. Boss went back to Bluefield and I went back to my
spot on the turnpike, though I did shift from Duanesburg
to a nice set of rooms in Charleston Four Corners, in case
of a wife.

So you could ask why I bothered to tell all this and there
is no reason, except it's true. It happened. Sometimes at
least that's what a story is, just what truly did happen and
if you knew it you could tell it. It might not mean anything but then what would? If we fell off the bridge, or
landed in jail for littering ash, or if we met Jesus Christ at
the toll booth?

I don't know. I'm not one of those guys who go off to
the Himalayas for sixteen years and shaves his head and
then comes back down to announce that Life is a Hockey
Puck or something of that ilk. Mama always used to say
I was a real rhinestone in the rough and I guess that suits
me well enough, though I can't say about the Boss. He
does act ignorant but you never know, he might yet have
aspirations.

Fitchburg Depot

Fitchburg is a fair-sized town but the Boston train still comes in at a simple uncovered crossing behind the Pullman Diner. It's flat land there, just a clearing in the scrub woods between old Moran Square and one of those sad new malls. People use the tracks as a shortcut—shoppers on foot, or teenagers holding hands—and somehow they always seem happy passing through.

My wife says it's the fact of Saturday; that young people always sail along happy and excited on a Saturday afternoon. Anyway, I enjoy being a witness and I count it a part of my routine whenever Ellie rides up on the train. I'll drive over early, have a coffee at the diner, then step outside and browse the scene until the train arrives.

These are small pleasures I'm describing, I know that, though maybe that's how I got to age sixty-five without popping an artery. Confession: I'd rather hook a three-pound bass at the cottage than go traipsing around Europe with a binocular, or lay on Waikiki Beach dripping dishonest sweat. But this hasn't anything to do with me, it's only meant to tell about the fellow I met down at the depot last weekend.

I'd done my cup of coffee and was out in the breeze surveying faces when two young gents started a ruckus in the parking area. One was doing all the shoving actually, terrorizing the other, and for a moment I was afraid it could turn bad, with a knife or (these days) worse. And maybe it did, but not in our line of vision; they were continuing their little dance in the direction of Moran Square.

"Wonder what that was all about," I said. I didn't really wonder, it was just we two had ended up watching together, elbow to elbow, and it seemed only natural to speak.

"Trying to steal the guy's girl," the fellow replied, with a worldly shake of the head, and though I had seen no girls I did remark it was nice knowing there *was* a reason. I never like to see this random violence, or even a simple bully flexing his muscles.

"Oh yeah," he added, "it's all the rage now. Nobody gets married any more, they all just shack up."

"Is that right?" I replied, a bit hollowly, having missed his train of thought. Perhaps he knew the two young men, knew something of their domestic situations? I tried for a better look at his face but he had half turned away; only a thin meniscus of sun remained over the western bend of track, and the weak glare off his eyeglasses was my friend's most visible feature for now.

Our conversation lapsed, and I watched the woodland to the east for some trace of Ellie's train. Four boys crossed the track, laughing and kidding, and then a young couple carrying those soft white shopping bags, back-to-school clothes I guessed, here on the last Saturday of August.

"Look at them," my friend remarked. "Shacking up, I guarantee you."

Maybe I nodded at this, maybe I blanched. There was no telling what he might say next, and no stopping it either.

"She took off, just like that. Here one day, gone the next."

"Who did?"

"My wife," he shot back, surprised at my disingenuousness. Clearly he felt he had given me more information than I could recall receiving. "I lose my job one day and she takes off the very next, just like that. Never says a thing, mind you, just goes and shacks up with the guy. I'm telling you, marriage means nothing to them."

As the father of two happily married children, I might have mounted a challenge to his thinking. For that matter, my own wife, Ellie, had not found our marriage without meaning, so far as I knew. But her train was late, and a damp chill, a whisper of early autumn, had touched the air, and my friend caught me off balance when he said, "She might not come."

"My wife?"

"No, no, the girl. She didn't make the early bird, so I figured she'd be on this one. But maybe not."

"This isn't your wife?"

"No, no, just a girl from Watertown. A friend. She wishes I had more money but sometimes she comes anyway. We look at TV together, that's all."

"Well, what did she tell you?—about when to expect her, I mean."

"Oh you know women, they *don't* tell you. I could give her a buzz, but that's a buck-twenty and I'm out of work, you know."

"What was it you did?"

"She'll probably be aboard. But you never know. Slim damn never, hey?"

"It is the last one out tonight," I said, realizing as I spoke that I had lost confidence in what I knew for certainty, that Ellie would be with me soon; be herself; and we ourselves.

"She told me to sell my baby, that silly bitch. Believe that? Sell Tee-Bird? No way, I told her: walk. And she walked. Just like that. But I do not fool around with my baby. She is a gas-guzzler, damn her, but she's my baby and I'll keep her over any bitch. I cover her with a blanket every night, for Christ's sake. Just the engine, you know."

Well, he had really opened the box now. People like that will, I guess, if you let them get the momentum going. His eyeglasses kept flashing at me out of the cool dark. I checked my watch and was surprised as hell the train was only eight minutes behind.

"She told me get a job, but it ain't so easy. Sure, get a job, without question. Except they're laying guys off all over the country and I'm the one she leaves. Well just register this, bitch: Tee-Bird stays. Tee-Bird leaves with me, can't go without."

Involuntarily my eyes scanned the lot to make sure Tee-Bird hadn't gone without. There were half a dozen cars, including my own, but nothing like a Thunderbird. I canvassed the horizon, looking for a huge blanket I suppose, with Tee-Bird underneath it. It seemed my friend must have walked here, possibly (being down on his luck) from one of the cheap rooming houses off the Square.

"Here she comes!" he was suddenly exclaiming, and I swung back to see the Boston train come steaming through the scrap poplar like a wounded gasping cyclops. As it screeched and settled, I was looking through the windows for Ellie but they were filled completely with milling young men in rugby shirts, or somesuch, who soon came rumbling down the steps like a herd at the stockyard. More confusion as a family of four got themselves jammed in the doorway, and then there was Ellie after all, handing down a bag of laundry she'd brought.

She had her little suitcase too, and of course a book in her hand, and to me she looked so neat and small, she looked wonderful, really, and the sight of her restored me to the high spirits I'd had driving down from the cottage. There is an emotion that hits me every now and again, like a oneness with the world, a simple happiness that just hangs in the air sweetly. It's not *about* anything when it happens, but it happened on my way here and it happened again now as I looked at Ellie and was seeing too the ripe tomatoes in her garden, and the clusters of peaches come to perfection by the shed. But the hell with it, because it sounds, when I tell it, like nothing more than being hungry.

In the meantime, I had all but forgotten my new friend and our odd friendship, as it had come to intervene between the two installments of this great good mood of mine. We had nearly reached the car, arm in arm and all the baggage, when I turned to check on him and there he was right at my elbow and I confess to a real electric shock at finding him so close. But here I got my first clear look at his face and saw it was very ordinary, a face that would be hard to recall, partly for being so empty of expression.

"No luck?"

"No, she wasn't aboard. I'll try again in the a.m.— there's one comes in around eleven on a Sunday."

"Well I'm sure she'll be aboard that one," I said, as he strode on ahead, muttering, though he had seemed philosophical. I charted him as far as Main Street, past the old donut shop. Was he thinking about the wife who had just taken off, or the girl from Watertown who had not just come? Or something else entirely—his altered job status or his bosom automobile. Were any of these things real? Tee-bird?

"What's all that?" Ellie asked, jabbing me. I loaded her gear into the back seat and straightened up to appreciate her again. She had not run off, or shacked up, and maybe those were things for which I had neglected to give her proper credit. But I couldn't answer her question; what all that was I surely didn't know, barely an idea stirring.

"One of those people," I said. "You know, like the ones who see off ships in a harbor town. They like the idea of comings and goings, I suppose."

"He seemed like an odd one to me."

"Did he?"

Ellie just looked at me, her wry look, forty years running, and shook her neat little head. "Ben Paterson," she said, "It's a wonder you can walk through the world ten steps without me."

Devereaux' Existence

Harry Devereaux spends much of his time in bars. "I'm a cliché," says Harry puckishly. "Once fairly prominent and well-respected, but in recent years etcetera etcetera. I'm a symptom of the times."

Years ago Devereaux did the dance and recital notices for the now defunct *Evening Hub,* albeit that unworthy old tabloid carried a Devereaux or two solely as sop and filler. There had been no real gainful employment since his days at the *Hub,* but Harry felt fully established, as though the post he'd held was somehow tenured, an ongoing honorary chair, a lifetime ticket.

"I'm a critic," he would answer, when you asked what he did.

★

Devereaux stood on his toes atop a brick and rested his chin on the young woman's bedroom windowsill, peering between the cotton curtains with a sheepish grin. But the sheepishness was merely a habit of face, an expression, for Harry was having some pleasure and experienced a strong sense of belonging exactly where he was.

He'd noticed her an hour earlier at The Three Bears Bar, where she and a girlfriend were drinking Dos Equis; she had a presence—call it sexuality—that tugged at him right away. On this sweet and balmy night, all blossoms and breezes, why not follow her home and see what was what? And her apartment building was just two blocks away, close by and quite charming, set back behind a scalloped cedar fence on Fayette, where now he could happily inhale the lilac and quince as well, as he monitored her undress.

As suspected, the figure was excellent, excellent, and the skin like Cotswold cream. Confirmed! She knew it too, was sufficiently taken with her image in the mirror that she touched herself lightly, here and there. Ah, thought Harry, the beauties of la booze, the fringe bennies, that she should free this comely well-turned lass for careless dreamy self-caress.

The black sweater came off and, as anticipated, there was the white breast, unguarded. Yet anticipation took nothing at all from surprise or delight. The black sweater, the white breast, the nipple—a *good* idea, the nipple. How bland the breast would be minus that considered concentric garnish; minus the graceful decoration, the lively coloration, the everlasting elastic nuance of the nipple. And how *exciting,* moreover, with the nipple!

Genuinely moved, both by the spectacle itself and his own expert critique of it, Harry began to applaud. Dazed with pleasure, expansive of mood, he would lead the whole neighborhood in a heartfelt ovation to the nipple. Indeed the applause was so heartfelt, so sustained, that he could still feel the lingering buzz of it on his palms as it turned, and he turned, to the sound of sirens. Soon he was smiling at a jitterbugging flashlight beam.

He motioned enthusiastically to the police officers, coaxing them forward to see the show, only to note in disappointment that the curtain had been drawn. The heroine was still fetching in her sweater and jeans, but really it was not the same. She had lost much in losing her nudity, the careless glow of booze and hair and mid-May nighttime was gone from around her.

"What can I say?" Devereaux shrugged apologetically to the angry-looking policeman. "You're too late."

★

Devereaux is aware of his own existence, he recognizes a few of the problems. You cannot have—simply have—an existence, you must go out and *exist* it. Yet the matter of initiative is vitiated by the matter of alcohol and Devereaux is aware of this too, of his drinking and some of the problems that come with it—alcohol constituting a clean honorable contract with defeat by which it becomes possible, however, to achieve a détente with the anxiety which attends defeat, defeat having become nicely inevitable. Fate is the party of the second part in all of Harry's contracts.

Fate, of course, cost him his job at *The Evening Hub*, took him far from the grandeur of art and gave him over to the squalor of life instead. So what? says Harry. He never considered another job, having felt the one he had just about perfect. There were no slots in his line these days, dance and recital, and what would be the point anyway, with Laura gone and Baby Hannah.

Odd jobs for dollars, yes. (*Very* odd jobs, sometimes.) But existence is enough of a job for Harry now, it has become his life's work, requires all his energies. Where could he hope to find more energy, even supposing a job did come along, something fitting that is . . .

Devereaux has resided in alleys and cars, in basements of bars, he has stayed a week or two at your flat, by your leave and without it—less what we now call "homeless" than what we once called a "dropout"—and commonly he sleeps in hand-tailored silk suits of the thousand-dollars-and-counting variety. "Just a little affectation of mine," Harry explains.

★

"Oh for sure," Harry was saying. "No question about it, booze is the devil in liquid form. I rarely come to places like this myself. But sometimes it can get to be too much, you know what I mean?"

"I do," she said. "Sometimes I wish I would go out and get good and drunk more often."

Harry put her age at twenty-nine. She was a school-teacher who giggled a lot, a sweet consistent giggle to reward his typically laborious verbal flourishes. But no such flourishes now; now he was on the move, in plainspeak.

"I go along and do my job cheerfully," he said, neglecting to mention that his job was existence, "but then every once in a while I get sentimental and decide to tie one on."

"And tonight's the night."

"The Shirelles said it best, Mimi. How old do you think I am?"

"Why do you ask?"

"You see my hair—"

"Sure, but I can tell it's just premature."

"How old, though?"

"What does it matter?" she said, reluctant to guess, not caring, guessing forty. Forty was close. Harry's hair was white as snow but he was only forty-three, plenty of existence left in him.

"Thirty-six," said Harry.

"I knew it was just premature," she said, uncomfort-

ably, hoping he would now return to the droll style he
had earlier.

"Thirty-six," he repeated. "My hair went white all at
once, overnight, when I was thirty. I lost my wife and
baby at sea, in an open boat off the coast of Newfound-
land. The Bay of Good Fortune, if you can believe such a
broad irony as that. I said how infrequently I come to
bars?—"

"Yes."

"Six years ago tonight. This is the anniversary."

"You lost them?"

Harry nodded and paused to sip twice. Then looked up
with a lovely grim smile. "God, I am sorry. I've gone all
maudlin on you. You're a wonderful girl and I hate to
uncheer you in the slightest."

"You didn't remarry?"

He shook his head no. Devereaux did not like being
short and cute as a general rule, but there were times when
it could prove serviceable, and tapping into the unfulfilled
maternity of a single woman remained chief among such
occasions. Right now he made himself so small and cute
and vulnerable that the schoolteacher would have to wrap
him up and take him home to meet her own need. Sensing
this result, basking in the sweet warm humiliation of it,
Devereaux pressed for the clincher.

"You have the same eyes, you know."

"As your late wife, you mean?"

"As both of them, mother and child." He sipped. "But
please don't think that's the only reason I am so charmed
by you—"

"Harry, don't you think maybe we've had enough to
drink for tonight?"

"Oh I don't doubt it for a minute. But then what, you
see. *Then* what?"

Well then, of course, the bundling up snug and the taking home to cozy. "The sharp compassion of the healer's
art"—Harry quoted as they strolled—"Resolving the
enigma of the fever chart."

★

There is a grace below grace, Devereaux believes, that
comes with acceptance. There is a humility beyond humiliation, where humiliation becomes simply a way of life, a
condition. The essence of one's existence, one's grandeur
therefore, sole remaining garland for the critic now free-
lancing, eight years unemployed.

Brought low, one can love to grovel, even as at the
heights one loves to soar. At all costs, Devereaux preaches,
litanizes, we must maintain our pride, our sense of *belonging* wherever we happen to find ourselves. That is the vital
thing.

★

Harry Devereaux offers to tell me a story. A "true"
story, that has happened to him. And I listen up eagerly,
for I have just purchased him two rye and want my
money's worth from the little gent:

"This was years ago, in San Francisco, around the time
the hippies were invented in Haight-Ashbury and there
was all this fantastic cultural upheaval out there. But literally fantastic: cops smoking joints on the beat, hair grow-
ing wild from underneath headbands and flowered hats,
pretty girls throwing off their clothes and jumping into
the fountain at the Golden Gate Park. Two guitars in every
garage!

"And I was there as an observer, a social critic. To take
a pulse, let's say. And with all that was going on in those

crazy days, this was the single most startling thing I observed that summer in San Francisco. This was what got
me thinking.

"I'm waiting for the Geary Street bus, with one other
man. A handsome black man, reed-thin, bearing a slight
resemblance to the singer Chuck Berry. And on the bus I
observe him pretty closely. Soiled white socks—the thin
cotton socks—and a pair of worn polished loafers with
tassels. A sporty yellow suit with grease spots here and
there, and a soft red felt hat. Over his arm (carried, not
worn) a blue Brooklyn Dodgers windbreaker with
'Dodgers' in white script.

"Pepper-and-salt moustache, one gray wart in the con-
cavity of his left cheek. I observe him unobtrusively, wondering about him—a fascinating appearance somehow, yet
ordinary too. But where is he headed at the end of his day,
that's what catches at me, almost like a game. Home from
work? Off to his night job? Visiting a lady? He is holding
a blue plastic case in his hands, in both hands, and it occu-
pies him. He turns it over, spins it, measures it with the
span of his fingers. Finally he opens the case and removes
a cigarette. It takes him three matches to get it lit and
during this process I see on his wrist one of those clear
plastic bracelets that hospital patients wear, or maybe epi-
leptics. He could be en route to a check-up, or a check-
in, for although he carries no luggage he does seem just
that sort of nervous to me. Hospital nervous.

"Well we ride along on the Geary Street car and the
farther we go the more curious I get, and the fewer the
possibilities remain, until at last we are alone again—no
other riders on the bus and one last stop to come—and I
think, Aha, the fellow is a muggist, a thief, and fate has
made *me* his next victim. At the end of the line! I do not

quite believe this (the man seems so passive, so still and self-contained) but I don't want to be played for a sucker either, and caught off guard.

"But no, there is no violence in him, no criminal intent. We reach the final stop, the driver makes his U-turn, getting squared away for the return trip ten minutes hence, and my fellow traveler merely takes out another cigarette and lights it. He is staying on. Yanks his socks up, smokes the cigarette, crushes it out, shuts his eyes. When the trip back into town begins, he is fast asleep, and his hands unconsciously pull the windbreaker up to his shoulders, like a blanket."

Devereaux has concluded his story, and he reassures me that it is a true one. Not sure how to respond, I offer him another shot of rye and he accepts, before excusing himself for the men's room. While he is gone, I glance around the bar, a pleasant dusky room got up to feel like a ship's cabin, about half full and quietly humming, and I am mildly surprised that it is not early evening in San Francisco, 1967. The bartender arrives with my beer and Devereaux' latest rye, and gives me a conspiratorial wink.

"The Geary Street bus?" he smiles. I look at him, I confess, blankly. "That's Devereaux' Anecdote. He tells it all the time."

★

Devereaux does not always have the benefit of reflection in the morning, but today there he is in Mimi's mirror and generally speaking he likes what he sees: the imp, the critic, the boho-aristocrat. A man at play—with situations, with thoughts.

Is the citizen momentarily without reflection therefore without an appearance? Clearly not and in any case here he'll be, a cosmic whipstitch later, reflected. The thing is latent, that's all, like most of life's possibilities. The tree falling with no one close enough to hear a crash? Everyone's favorite metaphysical puzzler? Phooey. There is most definitely a sound, take my word for it, says Harry, reality is real even when you don't stop, look, and listen.

But perhaps, muses Harry on studying further his mirrored image, a man who eats yoghurt for breakfast is wrong to sport a beard.

★

Devereaux' trial took place in a strange basin of a room, a cavernous old amphitheatre with big bags of cold air rolling around the walls of richly aged oak panels. City of Cleghorn v. Harry Devereaux was called early, running through a string of quickies, simple matters to clear the docket. But the case proved imperfectly disposable.

"How plead?" a man asked Harry.

"How indeed?" Harry replied, pleasantly surprised by this quaint turn of jurisprudential phrasing.

"Guilty or Not Guilty, Mr. Devereaux. Are you represented today by counsel?"

"I am *pro se,* if it please the court, but I make it a real point never to plead. *Asking* is okay, but pleading never. But I can say with complete confidence that I am guiltless."

"Guilty? Plead guilty?"

"No, sir, guiltless. Without guilt."

"Innocent, then."

"Oh hardly, mon ami. Shameless, guiltless, aimless. That is Harry D. as he stands before you, mottoistic though she scan."

"We'll take this one after lunch," the bench interceded here. "When we do resume, Mr.—ah—Devereaux, please bear in mind that *you* are being tried here, not my patience. Contempt charges loom if you persist."

Harry, who had time for a short sip outside, decided right then and there to alter his legal strategy; after lunch, he would argue the case *sans perruque,* for that must be the problem. And so he did present himself—shameless, guiltless, aimless, and wigless—when after three excruciatingly long and boring hours he finally heard the city's attorney attempt to demean him in the weariest of voices:

". . . Defendant, moreover, was observed by both the victim and two arresting officers, including Officer Maguire who is in court today to testify. At the time, Defendant made no attempt to deny his guilt and I fear he is just playing games in doing so now."

"Objection!" bellowed Devereaux. "Object to the phrase 'just playing games' as being highly judgmental. Might also point out that on the night in question, night of May Twen-tee-two, Defendant was also 'just playing games.' And what of it?"

"Please continue, Mr. Mahoney," said the bench.

"Also object," Harry rolled on regardless, "to the use of the term 'victim,' the belief here being that the crime of peepage is surely a victimless crime if the expression has any meaning at all, proof being that ninety-nine times out of a hundred the so-called victim doesn't even know the so-called crime has occurred. When you are *mur*dered, bo, you *know* it."

"Surely not always?" said the bench, looking mildly interested.

"Your Honor," said the city's attorney with some urgency, considerably less weariness in his voice. "Perhaps it would be best if we proceeded with the witness now?"

"Mr. Devereaux?"

"Your Highness?"

"'Your Honor' is probably the usage you want, Mr. Devereaux. Do you have any objection to our proceeding with the evidence now?"

"Call Officer Maguire!" trumpeted Harry and sure enough, as though by magic, the man Maguire materialized. But he would need careful handling; he sat on the stand with a nervous angry air, an air of feeling totally in command and badly out of place, both at the same time. "In your opinion, Officer Maguire, did my client show any sign of guilt upon apprehension? Any hint of wrong-doing?"

"Sure you did. You were peeping right in the young lady's window there."

Here Harry was reeled in briefly, and instructed that before he went ahead with his cross-examination he must first allow the prosecution a word with its witness. So he was forced to audit Maguire's unimaginative and halting account of the 'facts' before he could have at him again.

"Now, Officer, you do concede that my client made no attempt to escape, nor even to mitigate?"

"I had you dead to rights, you little devil."

"Do you affirm or deny that my client, at the time of apprehension, appeared shameless, guiltless, aimless?"

"He was too drunk to run, Judge! I'm telling you—"

"That's fine, Officer Maguire, no need to worry now. Mr. Devereaux, we are all glad to see you having some fun, but the court does have other business. I must ask you to leave off your pursuit of metaphysical guilt and stick to the statutes just briefly—the *statutory* definition of guilt and innocence. Have you anything to argue on that score?"

"I might. But I have begun to feel that a jury trial may prove necessary to my case. I am sure that twelve of my peers, twelve honest men and true, would at once see the absolute *normalcy* of my alleged behavior. The true givers of the law—"

"I'm afraid we don't hold jury trials for misdemeanors. And, please. If you are considering a plea of temporary insanity—if you have that one cranked up in the bull-pen?—it won't wash for the same reason. Why don't we just fine you and let it go at that. Wouldn't that be fair?"

"Fair? If you had been there that night, with me at the window, Your Honor would know this was no criminal act. The farthest thing from it. You would see it was a good thing, a very nice thing, it was part of my sex life, it was *okay*."

"It was not okay, Mr. Devereaux. This Court fines you one hundred dollars as a first offender. Please make arrangements to pay before you leave the building, and please try not to involve anyone in your sex life without their knowledge and approval in the future. Understood?"

"No," said Harry unwavering. "On behalf of my client I shall appeal, and I shall further instruct my client to pay no fine until every path of appeal has been exhausted."

So it was that Harry, in his forty-third year to heaven, spent a little time in stir, drying out.

★

She was neither young nor pretty; she wasn't even that nice. Plus, he had caught an undercurrent of disapproval coming from her even as she listened and bought the drinks. It occurred to him that hers was the behavior of a degree candidate in the social sciences, out doing a spot of nasty research for her thesis.

Still, it was time to choose between retreat and escalation, time to weigh in such factors as the hour (late) and the weather (worst of January) against the woman's lukewarm willingness and somewhat marginal appeal. And more perhaps from habit than inclination, Harry chose to sail ahead into the wind. He juvenesced as pathetically as possible and launched straightaway into the account of the open boat, Cape of Good Fortune, lovely wife Laura, and the bright tiny jewel of his heart Hannah.

Truth is he had just achieved a trace of momentum—and momentum comes hard where never is heard an encouraging word—and had even strained his artifice for a touch or two new (with her ultimate breath the child had asked if this, death, meant her next birthday would never take place . . .) when the degree candidate shot him down like a brittle skeet.

"I happen to know your ex-wife, Harry," she announced, with an ugly triumphant game-ending flourish. "I know Laura, she's a friend of mine. I know Hannah, too, the jewel of your heart who you didn't have the decency to phone at Christmas—or for the five months prior to Christmas, either."

And Harry started to fall, flat and hard and totally broken, like that skeet. But no: he had his pride, he was not such an easy target. He might have explained (for what could she know, Little Miss Entrapment, all smug and false, about the difficulties he faced, the twisting of so many rusty blades in his poor dyspeptic belly) but pride stopped him there too. Instead he breathed.

"Ah," he said, finally. "You know my wife. I hope you

will remember me fondly to her next time you see her, and let her know I'll be by soon to say hello in person."

Then he stood unsteadily and swivelled, reached back for his drink with a grace below grace, and repaired to a neighboring table, altogether jaunty in the face of despair.

Fishing for Gorillas

Chapman did not exactly wake up, since he was not exactly asleep. Exact sleep was something that had eluded him lately. Still, there was a transition to be handled, from the warm oblivion of his bed to the cold oblivion of the kitchen, and quickly, if he hoped to have ten precious minutes of tranquility.

It was not to be. Chapman had dug out two socks of the same approximate color, but the coffee was just starting to percolate when the first sputtering sounds filtered down the hall from Bessie's room. He knew there was no riding it out, for any delay would only cause a terrible momentum to gather, the sputters expanding to howls, the howling to a bestial roar.

"Bessie, Bessie, I'm right here," he said, scooping her in his arms and hushing her softly. Almost at once she subsided, to sobbing, then to a decrescendo of gasps and glottal hiccoughs, finally a rhythmic labored breathing: she was awake.

"I dreamed a gorilla," she said.

"The same way?"

"Yes. We were fishing, like at the lake that time, and you said watch out behind me when I threw the hook, and then I felt him tugging—"

"Did you pull him up this time?"

"A little. I saw his big gorilla head come out of the water and then you came for me."

"Well he's gone now," said Chapman, stroking her narrow little back. She understood about dreaming, that there was no gorilla, the gorilla was not real—but neither was he altogether unreal. Traces of him would remain until the jolt of cold fruit juice, hot hit of milky tea.

They raced down the hall now to stop the coffee from burning, and he settled her into her chair.

"Flakes or Pops?" he asked.

"Krispies."

"No Krispies, Bess. Remember? We finished them."

"You can get more."

"I know, queenie, but so far I didn't, so there we are. Flakes or Pops?"

"Opameals."

"No oatmeal either. If you really want some hot cereal, I can make you farina."

For some reason she assented to this, and Chapman put the water up to boil, then sliced into a melon for her. She gnawed two wedges thoughtfully before asking,

"Are antelopes called antelopes because they eat cantaloupes?"

"Yes, Bess."

"That's what I thought."

He was looking at the paper now, not with the sort of mindless enjoyment he preferred, but with anxious glances, almost furtively. Even this modicum was soon denied him, for she had coaxed the farina onto her lap. "Messy Bessie," she said, philosophically.

"You took the words right out of my mouth."

"I did *not!*" she laughed hotly, amazed he would give voice to such a bizarre notion. "It burns my leg."

She appeared thoughtful again as he tidied her up, rinsing the nightgown and draping it on the shower rod to dry. At least he hadn't dressed her yet.

"Will my mama die?" she said, as he was pulling the undershirt down over her head. When her face came through the hole, he kissed it. She had asked this already.

"No, angel, she won't die."

"Will she walk home from the hospital when she's ready?"

Nan had said this, of course—that she would just walk home from the hospital when she was good and ready—but it was a grimly conjectural business. The doctors simply did not know what was wrong with her, why her legs could not move. They were very reassuring in tone, but it could not be reassuring that such faith had no apparent medical basis.

"I dreamed we were all fishing once, you and me *and* Mama. Fishing for *fish!*"

"You never told me that one," he said, pretty sure this was invention, and that she no longer cared to risk an answer to her question, still hanging in the air.

"I forgot," she shrugged.

"Okay, little one, you're almost set to go. It's late, so I think we'll let Mrs. Cowden brush your hair."

"I want *you* to brush my hair."

"Mrs. Cowden is a lot better at brushing hair."

"I don't want to go there."

"Yes you do, and do you know where we're both going tonight, right after we finish dinner?"

"To Mama?"

"Correct. So let's get the day rolling, and before you know it, I'll be coming back to get you."

He came back to get her on the late side, nearly six, so they wolfed down hot dogs and beans (and ginger ale instead of milk, because Tuesday is the cow's day off) and then they drove across the river to the hospital with a bag of books and a clutch of jonquils that made Bess think the books smelled good.

They parked and raced up the hospital steps into the high, hushed foyer. Bess was disappointed to find the gift shop locked and dark, but she recovered at once and went sliding off down the long corridor to Nan's room, nearly gaining the doorway before she remembered the books and flowers, and that she had wanted to be the one to present them.

Nan looked up pleased. Her face was pale, sallow, but her smile always gave it some life. Whether from the white light of the hospital or the disease itself, her blue eyes looked gray and washy.

"What luck! I was hoping you guys would come see me tonight but I was about to give up."

"It's only quarter after seven," said Chapman, exaggerating slightly. He kissed her forehead and tasted the unnatural coldness. It often felt as though she had just broken a fever and dried off, leaving the skin luke-cold.

"I give up easily. How's your day?"

There was no answer, for Bess now moved in and joined Nan in the bed. She worked the incline button until she had the bed curved like a worm, then bit into some toast on Nan's tray with unhappy results.

"I'm afraid that's been there a while," Nan said, hugging her.

"It's yuk!"

"I'm sure."

"I know what crumbs are, Mama."

"Do you really?"

"Uh-huh. Crumbs are *crumbs!*"

"Well *you're* no dope, are you lovey?"

She looked over at Chapman with a glow, as if to say, She's doing fine, you're pulling both oars, but Chapman shrugged her off. The oars had to be pulled, of course, and beyond that there was no telling . . .

Nan shuffled the mail he had brought and found a letter they had been waiting for, from the insurance company. She read it and cursed them.

"It doesn't matter," he smiled. "I've come across the perfect precedent for simply ignoring the bill."

"That we can't possibly pay it?"

"No, this is an Oscar Wilde story." (Chapman had quite a few Oscar Wilde stories.) "Wilde doesn't pay his tax bill on time, so naturally the London tax collector appears at his front door to ask for the money. Wilde declines. The tax man is somewhat at a loss. He steps into the great hall, gestures at the lavish appointments, and says, 'But sir, you are the householder here? You do sleep here?' 'Ah yes,' Wilde sighs, 'but then I sleep so badly, you know.'"

"Can I ride the wheelchair?" asked Bess, overcome with boredom at the first incursion of grown-up talk.

"I like the story," said Nan to Chapman.

"Sure," said Chapman to Bess. "Just be sure to stop at all the red lights—and write home, you hear?"

"Silly Papa."

"Where were we?" said Chapman, as they watched her spinning toward the nurse's station, where she knew she could count on some attention and candy.

"She seems so gay. She was never this charming when I was healthy."

"I think she's all right. She still has the animal dreams, though—usually the gorilla."

"Well it has to come out somewhere. And it is all pretty obvious—"

"Is it?"

"Sure. The unpleasant surprise, the dismay and the fear . . ."

"Surprise, dismay, fear. And here I was, treating it as your ordinary fishing vignette."

"I know, Chaps, but still it's true. And it's probably very therapeutic for her, too."

"Gee, maybe we should enroll her at the Institute Of Gorilla Therapy, for a week of really *intensive* surprise and dismay. And you know, I'm almost positive the Advanced Dismay Seminar makes a field trip right here, to this very hospital."

Though Nan smiled at his lame academic humor, Chapman could see how weary she was, how slack at the core. The most impressive part of all this was that she actually had her sense of humor intact, and her poise. *She* had not given way to fear. Yet she must be very fearful, how could she not? After months with no feeling in her legs, months without knowing *why* there was no feeling, she had to wonder why not worse—why not her neck, her brain, why not death? The doctors were "optimistic" but then so were the chambermaids, whose opinions on the medical posture were neither more nor less relevant. And somehow Nan sat through day after day of it, cheering up the gloomiest of the nurses, ploughing through her Trollope novels one after another, shrinking by another pound or two each week. Perhaps she cried more when no one could see her, or felt the fear at night, in the dark; perhaps she desperately craved the morning light after all those hours alone with her own intelligence, but there was never the faintest suggestion of giving way. Instead, she worried about him.

"Really. You should get to a movie or two. *Some*thing."

"I will, but listen, they'll kick us out soon. Tell me what's been going on. Is there anything new?"

"Another day, another intern. My forty-fifth life history and examination. I'm a learning post, Chaps. This one had a wristwatch like a hockey puck—and he was extremely thorough in checking out my breasts."

"Oh Christ. Nothing new at all?"

"Not really. They want more blood on Thursday, if you feel like going through that one again."

They fell silent together, four hands touching. Chapman looked up at the clock. Then Bess wheeled in with two young nurses in tow, and asked if she could do puzzles.

"In a minute. Come visit with me first—I won't see you again for a few days."

"Why not?"

"Cause you won't be here, that's all. So come curl up with me."

"You smell funny," said Bess, with just a hint of cruelty.

"I do? Well, sit on the chair, then, and tell me what this Papa has been feeding you."

"Beans and lemon soda," she said, aggressively.

"Hot dogs and beans," Chapman shrugged.

"Yes, but lemon soda?"

"Cow's day off. Anyway, it was ginger ale."

"What else has he cooked, Bessie?"

"Nothing!"

"What the dear girl means is that she has *eaten* nothing. I've done it all—broiled burgers, boiled birds, fried fishes—"

"Yuk," said Bess, to the fish.

"I'm telling you," said Chapman, "it's like watching the Miss Infantile Neuroticism Pageant at every meal. Folks, did you know that I.N. kills more parents than any other childhood disease?—"

"Hush. You don't know how most children are."

"I don't? You do?"

"Two for two, Chaps. But neither of you knows how good you have it. Taste this," she said, indicating her tray, where sat the untouched fillet of cardboard in a congealed tan gravy.

"Thanks, no."

"The worst part is that all the nurses are so nice, and they *want* me to eat so badly. Ginny brought me some lunch today."

"How's Ginny?"

"Fine, terrific. We had fun arguing about something that either did or didn't happen twenty years ago."

"What happened, Ma?"

"Well, your Aunt Gin says it *didn't* happen. But it isn't a story you would like, honey."

"Tell the story, Ma."

"If you insist, O my best beloved. Gin was about ten and I was twelve or thirteen, and we were riding a bus to Vermont, where the Barnwells had rented a lake cottage. Ginny always got sick on busses and she was about to throw up—"

"Keep going, silly."

"—so I said I'd ask the driver to stop. Being her big sister and all? Absolutely not, she says, not one word about this to *any*one. So I told her that was dumb, the driver wouldn't mind a bit, probably had to stop all the time. Absolutely not, says Gin, and a few minutes on down the road she unzips her precious little blue suitcase and neatly regurgitates right into it—and that means throw up, O best beloved, right in with Stuffy the Bear and her seersucker sunsuit—zips it back up and gazes out at the scenery as though not a thing had happened."

"That's *gross*. Aunt Gin didn't do that."

"That's priceless," said Chapman. "And I'm sure she did."

"Well, we had fun arguing, anyway. She brought me rock candy, if you want something—"

"A *little* something," said Chapman, shaking out the candy for Bess. "But then we'd better let you rest."

"I'm rested, I'm rested. I've been resting for months."

"Some of the younger generation might need rest, too."

"I know," said Nan. "You're right."

She smiled and reached for Bess, who resisted briefly out of a purely instinctual perversity, then snuggled happily against her mother. Chapman kissed them both, and reflexively put his lips to Nan's forehead again; still luke-cold. Amidst a hail of arrangements, reminders, half-baked plans, and protestations of love, he bundled Bess away.

Outdoors the temperature had dropped and they both felt the chill deeply. They were tired and, now that the visit was over, wanted to be home right away. For Bess it was bedtime, for Chapman another long day without respite. He had dashed out at lunchtime to run down a sack of groceries and had vague notions of getting to some of the laundry after Bess was in bed. His purely personal ambitions had been reduced to getting cleaned up and then reading his way into a good mystery, preferably set in Miami or L.A., someplace warm and unreal.

They drove the beltway in silence, Chapman remembering the things he had forgotten to tell Nan, Bess gazing absently at the fragmented light slashing at the windshield. He put his hand on her knee as a replacement for the conversation neither of them desired. The knee felt terribly small and bony.

She was already asleep when he carried her up and dumped her softly on the couch. He wrestled her out of her clothes and into a flannel gown, then hesitated: would she undream the damn gorilla if she slept in his bed?

He let this one go. The truth was he didn't want to share his bed with her. Bess was a sprawler, a territorialist, for one thing; plus having her there always made him tense up and go sleepless with the effort to keep from disturbing her. The sleeping-on-eggshells syndrome. Anyway, the gorilla was good, the gorilla was *therapeutic,* so he hauled her to her loft, kissed her cheek, and covered her shoulders carefully.

Immediately he felt a pressure to get things done, to put his life in order, but pressured too by the need to relax. It was as though "relaxation" was on his list of things to do. He ran a hot bath in which he at least could read the morning paper, but it felt stale—it was not worth much as literature, not reading to catch up on exactly—and the pages kept getting wet despite the fact that his arms grew heavy with the effort to keep them dry.

He made coffee and brought it to bed, where he started in on a Japrisot thriller and finally did relax, or collapse. Each sip of coffee seemed somehow to make him drowsier, until the pull of sleep was irresistible and he sank down into it with the book spreadeagled on his neck. He was soundly, deeply asleep for two minutes, then snapped awake, his mind suddenly brimming with all the chores he hadn't got to—the phone calls, the sink jammed with pots and dishes, the godawful galloping laundry which was gradually taking over every room like a protoplasm, a cancer. . . .

And Nan's birthday, for God's sake. He was committed, *lashed* to the notion of getting her something special, dreaming something up, and now there was barely time to get her anything at all. The whole list was trivial, yet it riddled him and spoiled his chance at sleep.

He cleaned up the kitchen, then went to check on Bess. She had drifted back to the wall in an open-mouth profile, and with her feet blanketed together she looked like a big fish, a tuna. He kissed her cheek again and whispered very softly, "Fishes, Bessie, there's nothing in the lake but fishes," then climbed down, feeling slightly drunk or deranged from the long months of isolation. It was all such a confusing whirl, with no time to think, no *way* to think about it; certainly nothing was "obvious" to him, as Surprise, Dismay and Fear were obvious to Nan.

Now he thought of Nan and the nightmare she had been enduring, of Bess and her nightmares, finally of himself, as it dawned on him—though it should have been "obvious" long ago—that he'd had no nightmares, no dreams in all these months. No dreams of needle-wielding nurses, no gorillas, no cars going off cliffs, nothing. No bad dreams, no good dreams, no places, voices, or colors: dry of dream was Chapman, a blank.

He was staring blankly when the staccato sound, a low garbled grinding, broke in on him. It was like something stuck in a sink disposer, except they didn't have a sink disposer, and now it was definitely swelling, accelerating, coming from Bessie's room.

"It's okay, sweetheart," he said, stroking her brow, "we're just home."

"I had a dream, Pa."

"I know, baby, it's okay."

"Can I come in your bed, Papa?"

"Of course you can, sweetie, but let's get back to sleep as quick as we can. Tomorrow's another day."

"I know that."

He bundled her in on Nan's side, as far over as he could get her wedged with the extra pillows, but she rolled straight for the middle, gaining ground on the diagonal. Chapman was about to roll her back when he saw she was already sleeping, her eyes were moving underneath the eyelids, perhaps she was already dreaming.

The Off Season

The main street of Abingdon, Connecticut, where I
grew up, was then a block of gabled shops—one for hard-
ware, one for dry goods, another for books and so on.
The eight thousand inhabitants lived in woodframe
houses, most of them white clapboard, and the children
would never have dreamt of locking their bicycles. Today
of course, that Abingdon is an archaeological ruin, poking
up here and there from under the crush of what is called
development, a perfectly commonplace outcome. Now
the population is sixty thousand, and the casehardened
locks cost more than did the bikes themselves once below
a time.

But I am not setting out to tell nostalgic anecdotes, nor
do I wish to belabor the death of charm in Abingdon or
in the world at large. Actually the town is still attractive,
even picturesque out on Sandy Hook, where the summer
cottages are settled willynilly among gardens, small or-
chards, and sunny fenced yards. A ragged stone wall still
traces the two-mile beachfront back to the bridge in town.
I mention the changes not to criticize or lament, but simply to describe the way I feel when I go there, to a place
at once minutely familiar and altogether foreign, where
such crystal memories from childhood mingle with the

unblinkable evidence of growth, inevitable casualties of the particular.

I no longer have any direct connection to the town. My friends and family have all gone, one way or another, and the shopkeepers we knew by name have left the field to anonymous franchisemen at the malls. I never see a face I know anymore, even though I lived here from kindergarten into college, and twenty years ago knew every face in town. Just last month, however, I did for once bump into someone from my past.

I'd worked several summers at a waterfront restaurant called Willkie's Clam House. I was a bowtied busboy there and Lew Farrow was the elegant maître d'hôtel. Lew was a pleasant (though never effusive) man and a perfectionist about his appearance—the razor-sharp crease in his trousers, equally clean part in his neatly barbered hair. He always looked as though he'd had a haircut and shave one hour earlier. And he spoke with care, selecting every phrase in sequence, as he talked of the more interesting shows and concerts in New York City, which was less than fifty miles away.

Now I saw him strolling on the public beach, though this was two weeks past Thanksgiving and there were wafers of ice in the sand. He recognized me, too, or remembered me, and we chatted for about ten minutes before I managed to recollect the single most remarkable thing about Lew, namely that he had considered himself "married" to one of the waiters at Willkie's, George Papas, or The Greek as he called himself. The two of them shared a rented house near the water, and shared an antique canopy bed too, embroidered like a baldachin.

Their situation was unique. The "closet" was so all-encompassing in 1960 that very few residents of a suburb like Abingdon even knew the word. Ike had been President for the last eight years; a man named Ronald Reagan, with a soft voice and a terrific smile, sold soap on TV, 20-Mule-Team-Borax. But Lew and George were not clandestine, they were not defensive or apologetic, and somehow their disarming sense of humor about themselves elicited a tolerant response in an environment where they might have better expected a merciless riding. Abingdon was a village of well-to-do Republicans, after all, and none more so than Art Willkie, a portly little tyrant who wore loud pants and waved a golf club, a five-iron, on his dreaded kitchen inspections.

The staff was naturally drawn from a lower class, but that was hardly a guarantee of broadmindedness. We busboys were at the bottom: myself plus Dennis, James, and Slim, three brown men who would drive down together from Bridgeport in a battered white Fairlane. Immediately above us were the assorted waiters and waitresses: Big Ben, whose kindness increased with his consumption of liquor and Paul, for whom the exact reverse was true; Rose, who would re-total her tips all night like a child checking her piggybank, The Greek himself, and Marco, a dyspeptic Italian half the size of a jockey who muttered and griped on the floor and would crash trays around back in the sanctity of the kitchen. All these people and more— the women who served up the food and the two silent white-haired men who prepared it, Ann the cashbox girl (twenty-two, a sweetheart, my secret love), the Willkies themselves—all accepted the connection between Lew and George, joked with the two of them and enjoyed it. Perhaps we've underrated mankind, or perhaps it was just a rare exception, but not even Marco, a macho man with a chip on his shoulder the size of a glacier, undertook to fear, despise, or belittle what the two men were.

Twenty eventful years had evaporated since I'd last seen Lew Farrow, yet his every hair was in its rightful place—he had been to the same barber again this morning! And it was the same iron gray shade, so that now at age fifty-five, as then at thirty-five, Lew looked precisely forty-five. Unchanged. And I wondered if they could possibly be together after such a time, he and The Greek, un-changed. Did such situations last? Lew did say he was still at Willkie's, holding down the old headwaiter post . . .

I wondered, but I didn't ask. Something held me back—whether fear of giving offense or just a reluctance to com-plicate the moment—so we shook hands, said a few more friendly words, and went our ways.

That night I nearly called from my motel to ask Lew the question I had not asked earlier. Sitting alone over a restaurant dinner—salad, pizza, red wine—I realized what had blocked me: it was that Lew himself had made no reference to The Greek. Now I was annoyed at my own callow recalcitrance and by the casual dishonesty of all social life. Besides, wasn't it even more offensive *not* to ask?

I found his number in the book. I looked for George there too and found no listing, but of course it could have always been that way. I didn't make the call, finally, be-cause telephoning felt wrong. It would be better to run by his house in the morning, or maybe stop for lunch at Willkie's, on my way out of town. But the matter took care of itself.

My reasons for returning to Abingdon are slightly obscure to me, especially as I neither expect to nor do enjoy these very occasional visits. Whatever the reasons may be, I find them well served by long walks on the wintry beach in what resort towns call the "off off-season," and I had gone for a last such ramble the next morning. I was coming up from the deserted marina—gaspump and gear at the boathouse, the floating docks on drums, rope-and-plank gangways—when I spotted them. They were headed across a wide stretch of pale grass and shallow snow between the boatyard and the beach, Lew walking behind in his immaculate polo coat and George riding along in a wheelchair, with a rustcolored shawl wound round his neck, blankets stacked on his lap. The Greek had always kept himself, by whatever means, a deep golden brown, burnt honey, which I associated illogically with the heavy scent he used; standing with him, you could not be unaware of either detail. Now, from a distance, he seemed to have faded several shades to a waxen jaundiced version of the tan, but it was clearly George—the dense black hair, thick continuous brow, and that worldly side-of-the-mouth smile to which he would frequently affix a remarkably sonorous, flirtatious click.

They were on the boardwalk when I caught up and startled them out of some trance or thought, a mutual yet separate inwardness, with both of them gazing out on the slate-gray waves and the cold lowery sky. I was intruding but I wasn't sorry, not after yesterday; anyway The Greek looked up and laughed.

"Hey, how about it. Luigi told me he ran into the kid. How's the kid doin'?"

"Not too bad. It's nice to see you again, George—I was thinking about you after I met Lew yesterday."

"Colder than Miss America's left tit, isn't it, kid. And will you look at that, not a body out there. Fourth of July now you need a pair of wings to get to the water."

"The town's grown."

"You wouldn't shit me, as the sparrow asked the eagle."

"It's gorgeous," said Lew absently, fixed on the cold rolling sea.

"So tell me, kid, you still pushing trays? No way, right? You must be first vice-president in charge of the second vice-president by now, or am I wrong?"

I told him what my work was.

"That's all right, that's nice—you enjoy it, I bet. It's good to enjoy your work, dammit."

The Greek had always been voluble, very outgoing, a fount of loosely held opinions. I also recalled his habit of patting people on the backside as they carted trays past his station, defenseless. "Keep moving," he would say, with the blandest grinning mock officiousness, as he patted. He did it to me and to the other busboys, did it to Marco who cursed him foully and to waitresses, young and old alike, who abided it. No one ever saw him do it to Art or Bea Willkie, though we all egged him on to such a liberty. I could see that lovely careless enthusiasm for play in him still, but obviously there was something very wrong. He was pale and thin, and he was riding in a wheelchair. At close range, the jetblack hair was thinner too, and showed a purplish tint, from impurities in the dye.

"Yeah, I've got it. But what the hell, it's a great country. Here even a queer Greek can get The Big C. Listen, it's okay, it's the fucking land of fucking opportunity."

"Cancer? How serious, George?"

"Serious? Listen, kid, how serious is death? Not *very*

serious, I hope. Like anything else, it calls for a few adjustments to be made. Right, Luigi?"

"Death?" Lew mouthed. "Oh yes, G., but let's not, shall we?" Whereupon he turned to me and launched a few well-oiled sentences on rays and chemicals, and hope.

"Oh shush," said The Greek. "Tell him the goddamn truth, Lewis. I'm dead, and it's just our good luck we never had kids. Did you know that Lewis never could get pregnant?"

I began to smile, then saw they weren't. If it wasn't a campy joke, I was not sure what it was. George looked bemused and bitter, Lew hurt or simply sad. I could feel the weight of their troubles pressing down on me, and the harsh doxology of the damp freezing wind. They might be starting a spat, or continuing one I had interrupted a few minutes back. It was time to go—I wanted to go now, someplace warm, for a cup of coffee—but just then The Greek asked me to draw the shawl in around his neck. Wind ripped across the open sand; it was beginning to snow, large slow flakes falling on the ocean. Lew gently touched his friend's head and looked past him toward the lifeguard stand, where a teenaged couple huddled together kissing in the cold.

"Keep moving," said George, in a perfect impersonation of himself, right down to the unmistakable leer, and Lew complied.

"Yes, G.," he said, and pushed off down the creaking boardwalk toward the shuttered pavilion. I walked along too, thinking how impossible it was to know what anyone else was thinking; feeling sorry for George, for them, even a little sad and sorry for myself somehow. We all were silent for a minute or two while the wind ranged and rattled inside the long train of wooden lockers, then The Greek began to curse inflation and the national debt and the conversation resumed in fits and starts.

Lemon Trees at Jaffa

From his desk, Paul Pollard could look down at the skaters in Central Park and follow their bright gliding coats against the cloudwhite ice. He loved this elegant overview, savored it, and its tranquility kept him from minding that his two o'clock was late.

It was a *pro bono* anyway. If the guy never showed, he would not have to sit there like Ron Weller, calculating out the lost dollars. They were all lost on a *pro bono;* it was wonderfully relaxing. He took the cases out of genuine interest and for the sake of variety, not charity alone; he enjoyed doing them and, unlike Weller, could put enjoyment before billability, at least some of the time. How much richer one was for having defended the former Miss Liberty Bell against a charge of lewd entertainment last month—a gal who could appear so fresh and young and pretty that Pollard half expected he'd end up buying Girl Scout Cookies from her that first Tuesday, yet who in full regalia could lift your wig five feet in the air.

He would not be interviewing denizens of The Fuckorama for this one. This was trivial and routine, apart from the coincidence of the name. He had gone through school with a Ken Busby. They had been friends, though it was Kenny who nailed the only A-plus in Howison's chem class, an outcome which secretly galled Pollard at the time.

They had also been part of a regular ice hockey game, twice a week all winter for several years running, and, watching the skaters in the park below, Pollard recalled those bygone matches with a wistful pleasure. The pond was actually a watertrap on the golf course—a perfect sheet of ice, oval and close to the road. They would hop the stone wall and waddle over the frozen turf in skates.

This other Kenneth Busby, the two o'clock, was up on a simple trespass, though there were earlier problems on the printout—trespass, shoplifting, an assault . . . Pollard gave a cough. The damned assault would make it tough. One might offer up the poor drunkard, pitify him helpless and paint him harmless, yet how was one to put it over when the fellow was not only helping himself to watches by the armload but harming—bless us and save us—a seventy-year-old gal at a bus stop! Almost peevishly he thought, Can't even a bum manage things more intelligently than that?

Then he saw on the sheet that the defendant was his own age precisely, forty-two, and Pollard knew. He could not verify it anywhere in this slim depressing file but he *knew* that this troublous Busby would turn out to be the other one, too, with the weak wrist shot and A-plus in chemistry. A long-faced, sweet-natured joker. A friend! How this could be so, this vast unspeakable change in their relative circumstances, Pollard could not begin to guess. He had heard nothing of Ken Busby in twenty-five years.

Quarter past two: maybe he wouldn't come. Pollard walked the room, wishing for the five hundredth time that the damned windows opened. And for the five hundredth time he was sorely tempted to fenestrate the space informally, by firing the J. F. K. paperweight through one of the tall plateglass panels. Of course he refrained. Sandra's face appeared in the doorway. "Mr. Busby to see you," she said.

Ken Busby was not the least bit surprised by Pollard, but then there was nothing surprising about Polly. He was right where you expected him to be. Busby was pleased at their reunion, showed no embarrassment regarding the circumstances. He was hale-fellow-well-met at the door and legs akimbo at the desk, accepting a cigar with natural ease and puffing it with considerable pageantry.

He was, of course, not entirely sober, yet he was no stumblebum either. He had wit and poise and the same old impish grin, curling up past two overprominent front teeth. He had exactly what he used to have, likability. Pollard was at a loss to begin. It seemed downright gauche to raise the legal agenda, or even to say most simply, How in the world . . . ? Kenny's comfortable demeanor made such directness out of the question *socially* and when Pollard did finally manage a gambit ("Let's start with some background, shall we?") he just grinned and waited.

"Twice before for trespass. Any particulars I should know about?" By which he meant, Please Lord, let there be particulars, let this prove to be a big mistake.

"Only that it oughtn't be a crime. I mean, really, Poll. All those large warm spaces and no one using them?"

"I take your point, legalities aside. But legalities are what we are facing here."

"And legalities are your stock in trade, hey?" Kenny wore a teasing grin, but Pollard was obliged to keep this part earnest:

"Forget the law, then. Call it reality—"

"Okay! In reality, then—reality as Hegel would have

it—I was poor and I was cold, on those occasions and more than a few others. And between yourself and mine, compadre, I may have also been moderately sloshed."

"But there's worse. Assault on a bag lady? Stealing watches by the pound?"

"In those days I was bound more by time."

"The hell. You sold them."

"Time is money," shrugged Busby.

"The bag lady?"

"Bad. Dumb. I was a slob. But Poll, this was not assault. If this was assault then so is a simple handshake. I took the dear lady's arm for a sec, that's all—gentle and kind of friendly, if you want a second opinion."

"God knows it may have been. The problem is that after a while the record takes on a life of its own—"

"But there is no problem, amigo. They send me upstate for thirty days, maybe sixty, all the better. The way I had it figured I'd go in right after the New Year and be inside for the really tough weather. I've got paperwork to catch up on anyway."

"You *want* in?"

"Let's say I am willing to pay my debt to society. But I gotta tell you, Poll, this system of yours could use a spot of oil. The way things stand now, I'll be lucky to get inside before March. Who needs that?"

"You don't care about a defense? Just going through the motions here?" Pollard never liked it when a freebooter failed to appreciate the act of charitas. It was far from unusual, but it always brought the taste of early grapefruit to his face, the sour surprise of betrayal.

"Yes and no. When I saw it was you, I welcomed the chance—hell, the privilege. And it is wonderful to see you after all these years. I mean that."

"I think you might. I'd be glad to see you too—I *am* glad, though I admit the situation tossed me back a few yards."

"Hey, don't let it get you down, Poll."

"But how can I help out? I don't suppose you'd take money?"

"Why not? Nothing wrong with money."

Pollard shook his head as much in admiration as amazement. If this was acting, it was worth an award. Kenny showed no sense of shame. It was as though all life's vagaries, and chiefly its disappointments, were a source of secret amusement, just so many wry moments; or as if the two of them embraced, and were casually batting around divergent but equally sound sociological perspectives. Yet Kenny was a vagrant. His hair was a wig of string and grease, his clothing soiled, frayed and ill-fitting, his uncut fingernails had trapped half the grime of lower Manhattan. He was habituated to lounging in prison. What could one say to him, knowing any sermon would be cleverly deflected or cavalierly dismissed?

"Say I give you a couple hundred bucks. Will you get yourself some decent clothes and a haircut?"

"The clothes, for sure. Boy, a good coat would be a lovely thing to own right now. But I better level with you on the haircut, I can't see blowing money there."

"When was the last time you worked, Kenny?"

"Got a job right now. I can always get work when I need it."

"Where are you?"

"A rooming house, near the port. Just a sweep-up job, you know. Change a light bulb. Pin money."

"I thought you'd gone to college—"

"Two years. Got out after two."

"You quit?"

"More or less. See, I had a little drinking problem when I was younger."

Busby began to laugh, chuckling softly at first, then tossing his head back in gales of laughter until he choked a bit on the cigar smoke and tears came from the corners of his eyes. He shook his head back and forth gently, settling himself down, brushing gray ash from his lap.

Pollard tried to think, but only vague ideas, more like images, played across his mind. Images of Ken Busby's Manhattan, flophouses, benches, phonebooths to piss in; of his own Manhattan, theatres, heated taxis, flowers for Marya at forty dollars a dozen. Images from the past, the one they had shared—a suburban paradise of soft lawns and long clean beaches—and the one they had not shared, for now he recalled that unlike the others in their bunch, Kenny's family had no soft lawn, no two-car garage. In a town of sitdown mowers, they rented an apartment above a variety store. He had never been inside.

And Kenny had not connected with girls. That was why they had drifted apart the last two years of high school. That was the precise word for it, too: it had never been a question of success or failure, there had simply been no connection. Looking at Kenny, it was possible to believe the connection had never been made, that there was a void.

But what now? Call it a pleasant surprise, a smoke and hello, and let it go at that? Should he try to talk Kenny into fighting the charge? If so, to what end? What could he propose that would make a dismissal meaningful? Pollard tried to think. Was help called for here, was it wanted; was it even a possibility?

"Why not come to dinner next week?" he heard himself saying.

★

Pollard wondered what Marya would and would not do—he had told her the whole story, of course. Normally, for company, she would invest heavily in her hair and come out worrying it was not quite right. Would she invest and worry with Busby coming? He would be curious to see. Would she trot out Granny's silver service and the bone china? Which way would he do it himself? "Can you take Mr. Busby's call?" said Sandra's voice.

"Ken, how are you?"

"Fine, Polly, but listen. I don't know about tonight."

"Why, what's up?"

"Nothing, nothing. It's just I don't like taking advantage. I mean, you've been an ace, Poll, a true democrat, but you don't have to save me. It isn't necessary, really it isn't."

"Come all the same," said Pollard, relieved. "I'll be sure and have your favorite wine—Port Rancid '86, is it?"

"Shee, Port Rancid's a bit rich for my thin blood. How's about Fruity Surprise instead?"

"Fruity Surprise it is. That'll call for beef?"

"Sure. Either that or seafood—though knuckle soup is okay too. You're *serious*, Poll, I can't get over that."

"Just come and eat, Kenny, it's no big deal. Marya is awful about last-minute cancellations."

"You could drag some other bum in off the street to replace me."

"Nonsense. We don't get such a good class of bums in our neighborhood. The kind that could pull down an A-plus from Howison in chemistry."

"Jeez, what a memory. No wonder you're sitting on top of the world. All right I'll be there. But let me at least bring the vino, like a proper houseguest."

Kenny came not quite scrubbed. He was almost present-
able. Had he been a sculptor or a minor symbolist poet
his appearance would have been about right, for the
clothes were well chosen: a charcoal suit from Barney's
over a blue oxford-cloth shirt loose at the neck and a
decent polo coat, used but not ill-used.

Problems arose at the extremities. Busby's shoes tum-
bled from his cuffs like two footballs from Jim Thorpe's
day and his hands were assertively dirty, as though instead
of washing he had taken some pains to ply them with
grime. His stiff uncut hair was sown with dandruff and
his most recent shave had been timed such that he looked
disagreeably smudged, neither bearded nor smooth.

Marya was fine; she scarcely blinked. (She had not done
her hair, or had done it the way Pollard liked best—
washed, brushed, and pinned up simply.) The boys were
true democrats like their father and moreover were disbur-
dened to find the mystery guest pleasant and funny. They
were prepared to compensate, or to romanticize him, but
liking him removed any difficulty from the democratic
position.

He had not brought Fruity Surprise, producing instead
two bottles of a good Pouilly-Fuissé in string bags. The
trouble here was that he drained one bottle and was past
the neck of number two before either of the Pollards had
disposed of a small initial dose. Busby would fill his glass
to the brim, like a child pouring Coca-Cola at a barbecue,
then toss it off the same way.

Inevitably there were consequences to this, though not
right away. Busby could absorb a good deal without effect
and a deal more with largely positive results. He passed

through a phase where he was as bright and charming as if he'd been a famous poet after all, quoting from Kierkegaard and Nietzsche and referencing the work of an obscure Swiss filmmaker Marya admired. Busby had brains, of course, and had clearly engaged them, even as he was tumbling to the bottom of the social order.

But as Pollard noted that the transfer of wine was now complete—the bottles emptied, Busby filled—he noted too that his friend had entered a new phase. He slumped, hiccoughed, scratched himself absently; something in his tone made the boys draw back. He looked unpredictable, for lack of a better word, and in that sense slightly dangerous. Not physically (for Richard, the older of the two at twelve, probably outweighed him) but metaphysically.

"More and more," said Kenny, claiming to cite the poet John Berryman, and rowing the air dramatically with his arms, "the world is becoming a place I do not prefer to be."

Of course there could be no response to this, so, turning to Marya, he responded himself: "More and more, Mrs. Pretty Pollard, this *room* is becoming a place I do not prefer to be. Which way to the latrine?"

Marya had colored twice, first the remark and then the joke he turned it into. "Get him out, Paul," she said now. "Before he gets any worse."

"How much worse can he get? The wine is gone."

"Yes and in a minute he'll be eyeing the liquor closet and quoting Shakespeare on conviviality."

Pollard laughed. When Ken returned, half unzipped and weaving uncertainly, the boys clearly wished someone would send them to their rooms on some pretext. Pollard saw this, but couldn't come up with the pretext. Meanwhile Busby put an arm around Stephen and drew him close. "Flaubert," he murmured, "speaks somewhere of the lemon trees at Jaffa. Do you know the passage?"

Four Pollards fell mute before this astonishingly mixed display of erudition and crudity, as Busby went on: "That print reminded me of the Flaubert, Poll, the one of the orchard. The lemon trees are fragrant, he says, and if you stand in just the right spot you can smell their delicious fragrance and at the same time inhale the aroma of corpses rotting nearby. Something, hey?"

Richard and Stephen took French leave of Flaubert now, literally twisting free and bolting down the hall without benefit of text or pretext. On the lam. Marya sat riveted to the first remark, about the Bonnard print, which happened to be hanging not in the bathroom but above their bed. What had this man been doing in her bedroom? Pollard just smiled and looked Kenny in the eye, for Kenny was playing a little game here, a perverse little game to which Attorney Paul Pollard was no stranger.

"Do you know the passage?" Ken repeated, to break the lengthening quiet.

"Why don't we eat now?" Pollard said.

"Yes. I hope you care for roast chicken, Mr. Busby," said Marya brightly, blinking twice but quite composed, her husband thought with some pride.

Busby did indeed care for roast chicken and had gone back to work at being sociable while under its influence. He left off with lofty quotation and they exchanged light stories about Abingdon, the old home town. Sitting down to coffee, they glossed over the missing decades with anecdotes and came around to "the case," as Pollard called it. Kenny thought that an overglorification, but was pliant and agreeable to fighting the thing in court if Poll felt strongly.

The evening ended well. Kenny left, they cleaned up together, then Pollard took a brandy in to sip with the late newscast. He was in very good spirits until Marya came flying back from the bedroom with news of her own: two gold watches gone, along with a diamond ring worth two thousand dollars.

"Damn," said Pollard.

"I'll call the police."

"No, hon, wait. I'd like to wait on that."

"You think he'll bring them *back?*"

"You're sure about this? The things were there—?"

"Yes I'm sure. And so are you, Paul."

"Damn!"

"Help me understand this, Paul—you are going to let that guy take you to the cleaners?"

Pollard refused the bait. He did not understand, either, but he did not feel he had been taken to the cleaners. How could he explain to his wife that Kenny was only playing a game and that he therefore was playing it too? That it intrigued him. Calling in the police did not fit the rules of this game as he perceived them; on the contrary, it constituted defeat, precisely.

"It's guilt. Your freefloating *pro bono* guilt. But don't you see, hon, that this releases you from it? You tried to help him and the man stole. Stole from *you.*"

"Why, though? I mean if it was guilt, as you say, why would his stealing change anything? He's already stolen in the past—that's part of the guilty concern to begin with, no?"

"Yes, but now he steals from you personally."

"Bites the hand that feeds him roast chicken?"

"Paul, he is a criminal. You have to face that. If you don't or can't, then he's simply played you for a fool."

Pollard drew a breath, and tried to hide his regret that Marya's was the logic of castigation: concur or be diminished. "I'm afraid," he said with a gentle smile, "he's accomplished that either way. I defend him in one case while prosecuting him in another? Admit he has good field position."

"Paul. The man takes a bundle from you as a handout, then walks in here and takes more. Frightens your children. You can drop the silly case. Keeping that one out of jail might be a full-time job—and you said yourself he doesn't even want to be kept out."

"Right, but what *does* he want? That's the part that interests me. That's the piece I need."

"He wants to hurt you, that's what he wants. To destroy you, if he can manage it."

"But isn't it himself that he's destroying?"

"Oh sure, he's already accomplished that. Now he'd like to take a few fat cats down with him. This is a bitter, failed man, Paul. How does the fact you knew him twenty-five years ago change anything? Everyone knew someone twenty-five years ago. Someone knew Adolf Hitler when he was a kid. Someone knew the guy who shot the Pope."

Pollard could understand her excitement. It wasn't the jewelry, it was her anger at being invaded; angrier still because he was *not* angry. Still, he was not. This was no time to bring in the police or the insurance people. Pollard knew that Ken Busby would come breezing in to the office for their Tuesday appointment and they would hash it out together then.

Really it was as though they had been playing poker and Kenny had taken the first big pot. It wasn't the pile of chips that mattered, but rather the way the cards were played; because he was apparently quantifiable to Busby, while Busby remained unknown to him.

Pollard had rehearsed the talk till he had it well-honed as a one-act play. Kenny, however, did not appear on Tuesday, nor did he appear or communicate thereafter. In fact he jumped bail, such as it was, skipped out on the court date, and went underground, which meant nothing more than a reversion to form. Pollard poked around, but found it tricky going; the address Ken had supplied, for example, was a vacant lot, a razed block. And while he did locate a number of people who recognized Kenny's picture, and more or less knew him, they knew him by a variety of names and none had seen him in years. Or so they said. Had Kenny put in the fix? At least three "friends" assured him Busby had shifted his base of operations to the warmth of Miami years ago and was most likely down there now.

Pollard doubted that. He took to looking for Kenny whenever he found himself out of the office; not searching in a concerted way, not making inquiries as in the beginning, just keeping his eyes open as he moved around the city. Sooner or later he'd see him. He strolled a lot and he could never help expecting to spot Busby at this corner or that, hunched over a coffee behind a delicatessen window. After mornings in court he would often stroll the Bowery, or ride the 1-Train down to Battery Park, where most of Kenny's contacts floated up. He liked to walk, to explore—The Excellent Dumpling in Chinatown, The Harwich Grille in SoHo, new treats—and to reflect at leisure on his cases. Pollard thought well on his feet.

He had begun to think more seriously about the law. Kenny's shenanigans had somehow provoked him, bumped him out of a rut, an inadvertent kindness. The law was largely procedural, it had that nuts and bolts aspect where one manipulated the variables to get a result, manipulated even the truth, chief among variables. A good practitioner would know how to win the same case from either side of the dock, to pillory the former Miss Liberty Bell or see her absolved in the matter of her lewd entertainments down at The Fuckorama. Now, however, Pollard raced past the machinery of a case, he pursued the fundamental principles as if each time preparing to compose a majority opinion for the highest court, that would itself be tantamount to law.

Yet he did this to no purpose, felt no moral calling; it simply happened. He had not got religion. The inspiration was more like the inspiration a painter might feel, to approach the thing and grapple with it. To be engaged. He no longer remembered the well-rehearsed talk he'd prepared for Kenny, but thought perhaps he had taken a big pot of his own nonetheless.

Other side effects were less beneficial. Ron Weller suggested one day that Paul could use a break, a week away from New York, even a "sabbatical" if he needed it. A week later, Ed Kronstein made the same kind offer. Plus, the surfacing of Busby (and his subsequent resubmersion) had left a small but unfortunate distance between Pollard and Marya. For the most part she was resigned, but she could not help hashing over the theme each passing week. Kenny might be *dead,* was her latest. Someone like that could so easily stumble off a wharf and drown, or get himself torched by hooligans. How wasteful, then, to be shielding him at their own expense.

Pollard could not imagine that Kenny had drowned or burned. He did recall his own surprise that night at dinner, when he saw how much *worse,* how frail and aged Kenny looked in decent clothes. But he knew things were better now—that Ken had food, lodging, maybe even hope. Maybe he *was* in Miami, stretched in the sun with a volume of Nietzsche or the poems of Baudelaire.

One day in March Pollard got his invitation to the class reunion picnic, back on the beach in Abingdon. It was official: twenty-five years. They hoped everyone would be there, hoped everyone would send in twenty bucks. So Ken Busby was a stalking horse for the past recaptured, the long unexamined book of it reopened. Recalling the names and faces of other friends he had not seen in decades, Pollard signed on, happily enclosed his share of the beer money.

He could not imagine the heat of July, or the horde of middle-aged highschoolers, balding and gray. He could not focus on the present either, and was relieved when Al Jacobs—a fine man, a good client—finally left him in peace. He was drawn immediately to the window and gazing down at the ice rink he found himself gazing right down the tunnel of real time to the pond where those boyhood games were played. Found himself actually *seeing* the wall of round cemented stones that bordered the course, seeing the loosebarked sentinel elms at the gate with their dark heavy curving limbs, and the green slatted bench where they stacked their schoolbags and shoes.

He could see Scott Wilson looming tall between the lumped jackets that defined the goal, and Kenny Busby, the shy and gangly jester of the bunch stumbling down right wing to try that familiar wobbly wrister of his. Pollard saw himself too, sailing in behind so the rebound came straight out to his stick as though magnetized—

This *happened,* he marvelled, just as surely as the inauguration of John Kennedy happened the same week; this too was an actual historical occurrence. So very long ago (the ice-cloudy texture of the day, and soon the fogging-down dusk) and yet he could feel the distinct heft of the rubber puck as he snapped a shot past Scotty's glove to tie the game before dark and dinner. He could see Kenny turn toward him with that goofy smile, rabbit's teeth, as they went into the timeless half-mocking celebration, hockey sticks upraised.

Now as he swivelled back from the darkening glass, Pollard was returning Kenny's grin—or resuming, after a vast expanse of time, his own—and his arms were lifted above his head for he had resumed the ceremony, too, sticks in the air . . .

"Hare Krishna?" said Sandra from the doorway, puzzled, good-natured, arms loaded with files. Pollard's smile quickly thinned, then bloomed again, for her; his arms descended slowly, as though sinking in deep water.

"No," he said, "don't worry, I'm not that far gone."

The Lizard's Egg

Like any lawyer worth his salt, I have a weakness for words. Were it otherwise, I might have called this account HOW I LOST MY WIFE—a terribly mundane title—but it *is* the story of how that happened (how I came to lose her) and very little else, though I suppose if I don't tell you who I am and who my wife is (or was, that is) you won't really care how I came to it, nor sympathize a bit.

So I'm Cal and she's Barbara. We fell in love at Clark, Espenscheid, & Richards in Boston, where we both were working (and both still are) as attorneys, about halfway down the pecking order at the time. On paper we're the perfect yuppie couple, easy targets I know, but really we are very decent people, reasonably intelligent, mannerly, no threat to our seatmates on the subway.

Barb is even good-looking—intense, bosomy Barbara will attract a glance at every crosslight—though if looks were everything I'd never even have spoken to Britt Pomeroy, the sort of girl you only see when you know her. If *anything* were everything I would not have done, but of course it isn't like that, life is not a prospectus, I spoke and more than spoke with Britt . . .

I daresay I fell a bit in love with her, for I am not terribly experienced, if you know what I mean, and these things may take on more importance than they ought. Let's just say that Britt was clearly something to me that Barbara was not, never had been, never would be. Still, I doubt I would ever have "gone off" with Britt (or she with me) and so I might never have lost my wife at all had I reacted differently to Sugar Ray Davis at the critical moment.

I'll get to Ray shortly (my whole unwholesome saga makes but the briefest brief, and might also have been called *IN RE* SUGAR RAY) but let me first set the scene at Britt's place of residence. She is single, in her early twenties, and shares a house with quite a mixed flock. It isn't literally shared, like a Sixties' commune, but there is a sort of dormitory looseness to it, an air of friendship and openness, such that they tend a common garden, cook out most summer evenings, come and go freely through one another's doors.

There are a couple of couples (one gay), a single mother with her son, and six others unattached, including Britt herself and the fellow with a cot and a hotplate in the cellar, called Carburetor Man. He always smiles (shiny white teeth through the greaseblackened face) but he never speaks, just emerges from below cradling the latest rebuilt carburetor like a heart ready for transplantation.

Knowing them only in summer, in odd abbreviated outfits, with their guitars and marijuana, I found these people slightly out of step with the times, half a generation out actually, except for Britt (in law school, clerked for us June through August) and the Davises. They are the mother and son, Carla Davis and her boy Ray—a tall, handsome black woman in her thirties and the most independent nine-year-old in semi-captivity. Nine going on nineteen. Carla "allows" him, that's the stated policy. If Ray wishes to do it, and can do it, then he may do it. So he cruises the city day and night on his bicycle, anywhere and everywhere—

Chinatown, the M.F.A., Harvard Square of course. Gets himself into Fenway Park for free somehow.

Last August when Britt and I were meeting twice a week, we met there, at her house, and I became a marginal furnishing in the general collection. Sugar Ray would poke his head in any time the door was unlocked—any time we were not *in flagrante*—as he and Britt were great pals. He had a charming little crush on her, and vice-versa for that matter. We never went "out" as such, but we often walked à trois to the corner variety for ice cream sticks, Ray and I being solid creamsicle citizens, Britt inexplicably drawn to the lime popsicle. And one time we did take Ray for a swim at the city pool, this my moment of great daring. Not at the pool itself, where those who toil at Clark, Espenscheid do not deign to bathe, but on the dicey cross-town drive, where I tried to sit up straight and smile, though my eyes were darting side to side like those of the rabbit in Mr. McGregor's lettuces.

People were melting like popsicles that day, the whole city was just roasting. To step back inside the office from the afternoon "air" was like the literal shock of an old-fashioned birth, the boiling and freezing waters juxtaposed. It was the kind of day on which a pudgy jogger in his cruel rubber suit could get from 200 pounds to a trim 180 all at once, if he could only survive the four miles.

No one at the city pool was suffering. There we found some five hundred children (a dozen at most Caucasian) whooping and splashing in the huge turquoise rectangle, happily indifferent to collision, which was inevitable and frequent. It was impossible, really, to swim a stroke without encountering someone's cranium or clavicle, but Sugar Ray was instantly at home; this madhouse was one of his regular stops, pay a dime and swim all day.

Ray took it all as it came: the heat, the pool, me. Certainly he took me for granted, there or not there, all the same to him. Britt was forever trying to foster the connection, Ray in need of "father figures" and I therefore the great white father. Not that I minded much. I sometimes got a little kick out of it—maybe I needed a son figure. And the boy was special, though as I say so cool I couldn't swear he even liked me. I know for fact he never once used my name, Cal, always getting by without a name or else employing "the dude" by way of third person reference. As in, "Hey Britt, the dude coming too?"

And Britt would smile, first at him, then at me, and say, "Yeah, Ray, the dude'll be coming with us."

It started getting gummed up between us when summer ended and Britt was no longer around the office. We kept on, quite truly fond of one another, but we did so with increasing difficulty and decreasing frequency. Britt was back among her fellow students and I was back into the rhythm of rising within the firm. The simplest plans, so easily fashioned in July or August, became tortuously complex negotiations, awkward telephone chases. We fell off by degrees, to twice a month, to once, to nothing at all. We fell off full of protestations, and good intentions, and even vague hopes for a future resumption, but we fell off nonetheless, steadily.

I am sure I missed it more than she. She could so easily replace me, perhaps she already had. As the central figure in her romantic life I had always felt arbitrary, temporary, vulnerable. I am not a handsome man, nor even very forceful when you consider my chosen profession. Intelligent, as I have said, and decent, but at my very best I'd have to say underwhelming. Britt, though, was irreplaceable. For me there existed no options, no facsimiles, no shiny new versions. Without Britt Pomeroy I was definitely thrown back upon Barb's charms for any companionship or stimulation I might seek.

Which was best, in a way, for I had made the decision to stick with my marriage and there would be less success in the venture if the gulf between us further widened. The natural gulf left me adequate room to dissemble, during my time with Britt and after, whilst scrambling back. There was a difficult season in our home, to be sure, but at least the difficulty lay all with me. To Barbara life was proceeding apace; to me there were patches of unexpressed pain, swatches of a sinking vacuity and despair, as I slumped through a succession of desultory conversations and symphonic coffees at home.

We muddled through, in the usual ways. I buried my head in work, we buried our heads together in good films and bad films, in sushi dinners and steak dinners and blackened swordfish dinners downtown. We tried a case together and won it, and I had a good win by myself, before a jury and brought off with surprising style. Barbara and I were both liked and linked at the firm, so that we ascended the pecking order hand in hand, myself just a chauvinistic peg above and Babs directly underneath, in a wry reference to our very occasional conjugal *loci*.

By the spring we had risen to the second echelon of the letterhead at Clark, Espenscheid, & Richards—the Dirty Dozen, as it is playfully known. Barring all blood relations of the partners plus two instances of latent blackmail against them that were good as blood, only six names separated us from the bold twelve-point type enjoyed by the partners themselves. I had begun to think: Heads up, Roland Farnsworth, one more good win and I'm past you; step lively, Carol Goldstein; stand and deliver, A. David

Pemberton! I was very lonely during this time, yet some days I could feel like a terribly important player in the wide world. Other days I knew I possessed the wisdom and maturity of a fourth-grader, or a fool—but a fool on the *rise,* dammit, and that really can help.

Then came the day of reckoning. Ironically it was our best day in memory, partly because it was our first free Saturday since Christmas. After waking to a surprising and almost easy affection, we took a pleasant breakfast on Newbury Street and walked out into an absolutely sparkling May morning. The city had surpassed itself, had overnight drawn on this cloak of rich greenery and sun-brightened flowers for which there had been no visual precursor during all the long bleak months of lingering winter.

We strolled to the Haymarket, poking around the stalls there, then rambled over to the water for a light lunch marred by one brief, illusory mischance. Across the dining room I saw some light brown tresses arrayed against a pale blue dress and with a small spasm recognized Britt Pomeroy. The shock drummed heavily upon my previously blithe heart, causing me to rattle my shrimp cocktail goblet in its pewter harness. Then the woman turned and was not Britt—was a pinched and rather nasty-looking girl in fact—but the damage had been done. How Barbara managed to suffer this subtle affront so completely I am at a loss even to speculate, but surely she had: our buoyant good feeling was instantly dispersed and nothing felt the same, then or ever again.

Had that false flash passed over, or that isolated imaginary detail been excluded from my fate, the whole game might have played out differently. I might have reacted differently when apprehended a few moments later by

Sugar Ray Davis, or missed him altogether, but what the hell. I am not sorry and in any event it's history now—the history of how I lost my wife. The lizard's egg will hatch, after all, and out will come the lizard!

I hadn't thought of Ray Davis in some time. When it first became clear the affair with Britt was ending I did feel a pang of regret at the attendant loss of the boy. By now, however, I had only intermittent flashes of Britt herself and even these had faded. They still held the power to strike, as we have seen, but perhaps no more to blind.

I spotted Ray's bicycle as we were drifting past the Aquarium. I recognized the bike first, with its rusty orange frame and shining set of gears that had come compliments of Carburetor Man, Britt's cellar dweller. Ray was straddling the frame, watching an old man inflate balloons with a helium pump. A few of the inflated balloons, sailing on strings above the old man's cart, had noses and ears. So the bike, the boy, and then the horror: Ray swung around and started rolling down the narrow esplanade toward us. Steered past a lazy seagull, squeezed the brakes, and pointed me out. "Hey dude, I know you!"

Issue a firm denial? Look perplexed and issue a gentle denial? Stand silent on the Fifth Amendment to the Constitution? But really, imagine a man so weak, whether in his character or in his posture towards the world, that a child's greeting can utterly discompose him. I managed a sickly smile, an attempt that no doubt looked more like a picture of a man biting into rotten flesh.

"How you been, dude?" said Sugar Ray, also smiling, and playing the man-about-town. He did not smile a lot. I do not recall his ever having smiled at me before.

"Good, Ray, and you?" I said.

And that was that. Any chance to impeach his witness, to cast him out of this open air courtroom, had passed. Ray shrugged and kept boring in:

"Don't ever be to the house no more."

"No. Sorry. I haven't."

"I think Britt misses you, maybe."

He had not once looked at Barbara, not straight at her, and God knows neither had I. Now we each did and were able to watch her face going off in sequence, like a firework on a string-fuse, ffffffff sizzlesizzle BOOM! And after the explosion there came no flood of tears, no spoken recriminations, no revealed feeling of any sort. There was only ice, the exquisite oval ice of her face.

And Ray? He had flushed me, certainly he knew as much. There had been no accidental drift to his conversation. On the contrary, it had all been very theatrical and out of character. He was just nailing me, nailing the dude you know, though it occurred to me that he had never known about Barb. He had it all backwards, probably, thought I was two-timing Britt—and so he moved to shoot me down. Perhaps he felt betrayed himself, but in any case the damage was done and I am pleased to say I did my share of it.

That's right. I had not lied to the child, hadn't tried to make *him* out the fool. Not that it would have worked, but still I'm glad I spoke the simple truth. Indeed I felt so elated having finally done so that I quickly compounded the damage by opening up to him altogether. I touched his head, looked him in the eye, told him to send Britt my love. I said it had been nice seeing him and I hoped we would bump again soon. I had poise, I was almost transcendent in defeat.

Well, I think if you have a very strong physical tie to

your spouse you can survive an acknowledged infidelity—
though perhaps not. Perhaps what it takes is a weak physical tie, combined with a strong sense of tradition. I don't
know. But I do know that for myself and Barbara it had
ended, I had lost my wife. As divorces go, ours was surely
among the least messy and most depressing. We were both
young and "eligible," there had been no issue—not so
much as a dog or cat to custodize—and we were both on
our feet financially. Really the divorce was just paperwork, neither of us felt it necessary to even consider
leaving the firm. The divorce was in fact a relief and yet
this much is also true: had we not seen Ray Davis that
day, we might have remained married forever.

I did not go to Britt. For starters I doubted she actually
missed me. That had just been an arrow in Ray's quiver.
Britt felt like a long dead moment lodged far back in time.
I had often wondered what she saw in me, had felt—as
I've testified—arbitrary, temporary. Surely someone more
suitable had come to hand by now. I have always been
engulfed by this sense of my own unworthiness, not only
with Britt Pomeroy but also before and apart from Britt.

Except, oddly enough, for the one thing. I did like my
response to Sugar Ray Davis. I did enjoy that rush of
coming clean. Though devastated no doubt, I was also
thrilled to see the precise moment of pain and loss flower
into an amazing blossom of memorable pleasure. No big
deal to you—I do understand that perfectly—yet for me it
was the only moment in ten years, or twenty, maybe in
my entire life, where I existed so purely for myself, or
liked myself so well.

Moving Water

Annie Riley sat at the picture window, watching the road, drinking her coffee. The road was a twelve-foot-wide dirt and hardpan surface winding down one side of Blue Mountain; no more than a dozen times a day would a car, or more often a truck, come bouncing past.

Winding down an adjacent face of the mountain, angling raggedly toward the roadway, was a runoff stream, narrow and gentle most of the year, a racing torrent six feet wider in May. At Riley's, where the stream ducked under the road, there was a wooden bridge, four-inch-thick oak planks laid across the rusted iron beams that spanned the little waterway. All this was on such a small scale, so crude and so far from any real bustle, that the planks were not fastened and the bridge did not have a guard rail.

But it was a pretty spot, especially on the downstream side where the water pooled out into a shapely oval between grassy banks, before it cinched in and meandered into the swamp maples. The deep sunny pool had once served as a neighborhood swimming hole—"Riley's Pond"—with a high tire-swing and a sand patch laid on over the grass to create a beachfront about the size of someone's kitchen.

Annie Riley, sitting in her own kitchen, watching the

road, could remember the rallying cry, Let's go down to Riley's, and the crowds of eight and ten (generation after generation, going back to her own) but she could not recall exactly when or why it had stopped. Annie had never gone far herself; she had grown up in a house in the village at a time when this tiny cottage was home to her aunt and uncle; had moved in with her husband in 1960. He died in 1975. No one had come to swim in years and no one called it Riley's Pond either—the place had lost its name when it lost its social function.

When Annie heard the motor approaching, she naturally waited to see who would be going by, waited for the low rumble of the planks and the dust cloud that always formed, but instead the air had gone silent. Not a woman who talked to herself, Annie Riley did occasionally push out her hip, or make the faces that went with common speech, and a little bit talk *with* herself, which was quite different. It was like talking with the collie dog Mischief, before she died, or with Carlton, her husband, before that. These days she had to fill in for them, that was all.

"Curious," she said.

"Yes it is."

"Well I know it came past Harold Aho's and there's nothing else *between* me and the Aho place."

"I know it," she said, and then she heard a soft splash.

Her best look was from the tiny pantry ell, but thick honeysuckle curved up past the window sill and farther away, across the summer rye, the brush had grown tangled and unkempt. All she could know was that someone was in the pond—one person only, to judge by the quiet cleaving of the water and the lack of conversation. When the splash came it had instantly revived memories of the time before Carlton died, the two or three years of his illness when for a while there would be hippies coming to the pond, from God knew where, and swimming naked. "Ten yards from the house!" he would say and, too feeble to confront them, he would mutter about getting a good load of shot for the .22.

And Annie would be thinking, It's more like twenty yards, maybe twenty-five, and thinking, that gun hasn't been cleaned in so long it would either be rusted useless or shoot the shooter, and she would look at her husband and say nothing out loud. Just touch his shoulders and mention she was starting the coffee if he happened to want any.

Once he did go out there, feeling stronger and more agitated than usual, and he took the rifle with him. There were four of them in the water, two male and two female, and he waved the rifle and yelled about respect for private property and then the blond girl came up from the water toward him, naked and dripping, started over the uncut rye all smiles and apologies (though of course she was taunting him, Annie knew, flaunting herself in the face of his discomfort and fascination) so that he had to melt back to the house.

"Did you load it?" she asked, watching him settle the gun back in its rack.

"No, just bluffing them."

"Old pokerface. Pair of deuces, bumping up like crazy," she said nostalgically, consolingly, resting a gentle palm on his shoulder, thinking about the pretty girl tan from head to toe.

"Do you know, they could conquer the world like that. Just walk into town naked as day and take over the Town Hall when everybody ran off."

"I doubt it," she said. "Sheriff Hatch would stand his ground and clap them in irons. Especially that blond one."

Annie didn't mind if this was a naked person, now. Nor

did fear occur to her. If it was to be crime, there wouldn't be any splashing in the water and as far as someone taking a swim, she couldn't see objecting. Why begrudge a swim to someone hot and happy? With her it was more a matter of curiosity.

Minutes later, she saw a red pickup rattling past the house, a young man with slicked-back hair and no shirt at the wheel. "That was it," she said. "Jumped in the pond after work on a hot day. What else?" But for the first time in years she considered the clean grass-smelling water flowing over warm flat rocks and thought of herself swimming, on a distant summer's day or maybe on a warm day later this very week. Maybe tomorrow, why not?

"Wonder why I never do," she said.

Same time the next afternoon, she remembered the swimmer and realized the day had trickled away. Half past four. Earlier, around noontime, she considered wading in for a dip, but it drew her interest only as an idea. The truth was that ninety degrees or no ninety degrees, she wasn't that hot and had no desire to be wet all over. "Age, it must be," she said. "Sure. What else?"

Then she heard the truck bouncing down the hill, waited and heard him crash the water. Must have slipped in from the bank yesterday, jumped off the bridge today, she concluded. And it was him going by shortly thereafter, black hair plastered to his head and so careful not to look sideways to the house that went with the water. "I ought to be angry, I suppose."

She wasn't, though, any more than she was hot. In fact the next morning she clipped back the honeysuckle and hacked away some of the brush around the pond. She hoped the changes didn't show—wished the Samuels boy was mowing today so it would look like normal upkeep—but she also did drop a beach towel on the grass between the house and pond, why she could not say. To warn him off, or wake him up?—or maybe again, just to normalize the cuttings.

"Maybe to say hello!" she said later, when he was there, because he looked so hot and dusty beforehand that Annie wanted to bring him out a can of Budweiser, and looked so cool and clean afterward that she could as easily fetch him hot coffee, sit him down for a chat. He was nice enough to look at, slim and muscled, and he swam in blue-jean shorts; just peeled off his shirt, tossed his socks and shoes, and jumped in with his pants on.

"You could hardly have him for coffee *without* pants," she said, and then, feeling naughty, "though some people probably do drink it that way."

"I take mine with milk and sugar," she replied.

Every day it was the same. She listened for the clatter of the pickup, it arrived on a schedule the trains could be proud of, he parked off in the pine needles and plunged in for his bath. He never took soap into the water—one reason she liked him, he had respect—but she knew it was his bath because of the way he ruffled his hair and rubbed his arms. There was a house going up on the Newmarket Road, she had heard, and maybe he was one of the ones building it. In the back of his truck there were always sawhorses and shovels, bags of material, sticks of lumber; plus of course he never came by on a Sunday.

The builder never altered a thing and neither did Annie, though she felt he *should* ask about using the pond, that it was only appropriate, as he could see this was not exactly the wilderness here. He never did, though, never even looked in the direction of the house; just boldly made himself the owner of the water and made her, the deed-holder, feel furtive and a little guilty.

It was on a Thursday, after six weeks of this, that he missed the appointed time. Annie was naturally let down. To her it had no better meaning than any other tick of the clock, but no lesser one either. It was as though a day went by and four-thirty never happened. She caught a strangeness from that, and a sense of being cheated, slightly. Then she guessed he might be sick (or worse, injured on the job) and wished she had been nicer to him, had *brought* him the beer instead of just thinking about it.

He wasn't sick, though, or hurt. A few days later she decided he was finished with the job, that was all. They weren't going to be out there on the Newmarket Road forever building the one house and maybe that was how long it took, six weeks. Anyway, three misses stretched out to six and so on, until after two weeks she was certain he wouldn't be back again.

"Too bad," she said, then quickly replied, "But why say that? What's it matter, really?"

True enough. It was something she had come to like, to look forward to and even consider briefly in the evening once or twice, yet it was a small, a very minor matter. Soon enough it would be too cold to go in the water anyhow, for July turned to late August awfully quickly these past few years. Already the afternoons were getting chilly in the shadow of Blue Mountain, with the pondwaters darkened hours before sunset. There were even a few red leaves reflected, harbingers, like the first gray hairs on a young woman's head.

It was September actually, a hot windless Saturday, when the builder did come one more time. Annie knew it was once more only—true she'd been wrong he would never, but she really did know that this was the one last— and she stood at the sound of his truck and straightaway started pacing nervously between the kitchen and the picture window. She went back and forth half a dozen times and then, without thought, she was out the door and bolting across the yard toward him.

He was already standing waist-high in the water, shaking his head like a puppy. Annie had no plan, no speech ready, and as she came closer, and saw him glance up startled and sheepish, she realized how unlikely any speech from her would be. Ludicrous, surely, to offer him a bottle of beer as recompense for his trespassing! Almost to the grassy bank, she had no pretext for being there, other than the fact the land was hers.

"Don't you know," she said firmly—though the words came unwilled, sliding out from somewhere inside her and unfamiliar—"that this is private property?"

She said it simply because there was no other choice, no other sentence that fit in with her sudden radical presence there. The instant the words were out, they seemed to her harsh, undeserved (his face all innocence and apology) and for that matter unmeant.

"I just hoped it was all right, getting wet in here. Sorry if I was wrong."

Annie had already yielded the point of course and was grateful now to find there were other sentences she could say after all.

"Well, maybe it's good someone gets some use of it."

"Still, if it's yours—I should have asked permission."

"It's moving water," she argued. "Just leaks on down the hill. Probably no one should own it in the first place."

"I guess it is," he shrugged.

"Maybe no one does own it. I mean the water itself."

"That could be," he said, agreeable on all legal points and still apologetic, though he did remain in the water. It crossed her mind that maybe today, this one time, he had his pants off and must wait for her to leave; in a passing flash, she imagined him walking toward her, the way that hippie girl did to Carlton so long ago.

Then it came to her, clear as could be, that the builder did not really see her or hear her at all. That he was agreeable, polite, because it cost him nothing. He had taken over her girlhood pond in the same way—cavalier and uncaring. Yes, she had been fixed on him these weeks but he was oblivious to her, whether as a plot of land, a face in the window, or a real woman standing there conversing with him.

Not that he was evil. His life was right now, that was all, or soon. It was out ahead of him and she was simply not in it. Of course she wasn't. Yet it was somehow not easy to grasp the way she was not in his life when he was so distinctly in hers. And when she looked up again (maybe a minute later, maybe two) he was in the red pickup saying sorry, and thanks, and it had been nice of her to be so generous about it. He was not relaying any real gratitude, Annie knew, only flapping his gums on cue. She saw he had a small red rose tattooed onto his left shoulder, nestled in twining greens.

"No sense arguing," she said, and as the truck pulled itself up to the top of the world and rolled off, she was already nodding in agreement: "Nothing to argue *about*."

The Undertaker's Choice

We were gathered at the lip of Micky's grave when I finally began to wake up, and it was the sight of the backhoe approaching that did it.

The damned thing had dug the hole earlier, clean and square like geometry, and now it was coming over the grass with Micky's coffin. What I mean is you expect to see one or two scrofulous gravediggers drying out in the sun, or see their rusty shovels wedged in loam, but even more so you expect the old amenities: to bear the weight on family shoulders, to speak a quiet word, scoop a handful of earth, untangle a flower from the bouquet. These guys even had the dirt hidden, under a slick green tarp.

Not that it was their fault The Mick was dead, or even that I couldn't seem to get going in the right direction— could only think wasn't this one hell of a day to *be* dead, such perfect summer, so blue and bright. At the funeral home a tall bird with a mop said I was late, they had already left in the limos, for the church. There, at St. Paul's, I barely beat the doors closing, barely negotiated the woozy gangplank slope of the aisle with the organ rolling through that sudden cathedral dark; could barely make out the faces of family, though of course everyone was there, even the fourth and fifth layers, the New York branch, not to mention all Mick's tough pals from the foundry.

They had set up the box on canvas stretchers and the friar wandered around it with his pots of incense and water rites and the Latin incantations. Then he spoke a few platitudes about my nutty brother who he never met and who would never have stood still for one second under the ill-fitting generic tributes being ladled onto his contrary reckless brow. All the while I could only look at the outside walls of the box and see Mick perfectly alert inside them, grinning his cockeyed ironic grin, waiting to spring one more joke on us, thumb his nose at one last mass.

And then we were in Beaver Cleaver Hell, in the middle of some endless suburb the limos were endlessly gliding through, riding behind the box, and still I could not picture Micky dead, stiff under layers of wax and rouge. Now I wondered was he really in there, so *confined?* Man, did The Mick ever hate confinement! But no one had been permitted to look—too horrible, they said—so was there someone appointed, by someone else, to make absolute certain of these matters? Who was it? And another thought, my old man paid fifteen hundred bucks for that plastic crate. What if they figured why waste it; what if they sneaked it back to their gloomy barns, scrubbed it down and sold it again for another fifteen hundred, or even marked it up ten percent to cover cleaning expenses?

Anyway there we stood, looking at the backhoe like a tribe of mutes, and they made known they wanted us gone barely a minute after. It was my sister Jeannie who shook them off—ushers, or whatever they were—and peeled back the tarpaulin. On her knees, weeping, she started scooping earth with her hands. We all came to do the same and soon everyone's eyes were wet and red, though Jean was the only one whose tears you could hear. There was a lot of hugging before they finally packed us back in the limos, all except me, since my car was the only one at St. Paul's.

The hearse was now empty, of course, and the head of operations stood alongside it like a sales ace caressing his showroom special. I went up and asked if he happened to be heading back by way of the church, knowing he wasn't but figuring the price might include a few loose ends of this sort.

"Of course," he said, but right off, as though he had been waiting just for me, my chauffeur, and he gestured me onto the broad plush seat with such a gracious smile I felt something like happiness stir in me, though my brother was dead and I didn't know the man from a hole in the ground.

"Happy to ride you over," he said, starting up the big soft engine, and sliding out a spotless ashtray for me as we passed through the grillwork gates. It was preposterous, and yet to hear a human voice, speaking the most ordinary human words, made me feel almost human too. It did me some good. I hadn't said a word out loud since I hung up with my mother yesterday and now I felt like talking, even to the point of just making conversation. So I posed him the obvious—why a man would choose to do what he did for a living. A mortician and maybe a dentist are the people I would ask that question, out of genuine curiosity.

"Well, I always liked nice clothes. And nice cars! But it's also true my father had the business and there it was, you see. Before the War, I had intended on going to law school—accepted and everything—but when I came out of the Navy I found I'd lost the urge. And the business was there."

He looked over at me and shrugged: "My son is in with me now. The third generation. But today is his golf day."

We talked as we drove, back through Beaver Cleaver Hell, past a thousand houses with such simple lives inside them, or so I imagined, remembering when ours was. The talk never went to Micky, to his youth or the cruelty of his fate. It kept strictly to the undertaker's considerable pleasures in life. The golf games and the clothing, the Cadillacs, the house which was too large to keep up, even his newest grandchild, a boy, born in April. He mentioned the special pride he took in bringing his educational background to the business, as a third-generation Harvard Porcellian and his son again, whose golf day it was, the fourth such.

Probably I make it sound callous or self-centered in the retelling, but it did not come down that way at all. The man had a gentle voice, almost a bedside manner, and he knew what he was doing; knew how best to soothe the bereaved, never belaboring the obvious (which we both were powerless to change) but simply being comfortable in his own skin. And whether he really fancied himself a doctor of the soul as I have speculated, an expert at bringing comfort, or was just dressing up a grand obliviousness in nice manners, it came to the same thing.

"Does your line of work—does it inure you to death?"

"I don't know about *that,*" he smiled, maybe because I had struggled for the word. Inure. But I wanted to know, and kept after it. What, I asked, would he do now, this afternoon, once his Cadillacs were back in the garage and the last details had been checked off? Or did he have another one of these to do?

"Today? No. I'd like to get out to the racetrack if I can. They have some decent horses shipping in for the Mass Cap, you know. Bound to be a bit more excitement than usual at Suffolk."

"So you're a betting man."

"Hardly that. We might have a drink and gamble a few dollars, that's all. But why not? Such a glorious day."

I suppose I could have felt offended by the remark. I did think how all remarks, all words and thoughts, will reverberate so differently on a day like this one. But I was not offended, I *knew* it was a glorious day, and asked who he liked in the race, God knows why. The Mick would gamble some, more dogs than horses, but I had not been anyplace like that in years. Hadn't even noticed today was the Mass Cap, and the names of the animals had less meaning to me than a list of the twenty-eight flavors.

"Dixieland Band, naturally. He's the undertaker's choice!"

At a proper jazzman's funeral in New Orleans, he explained, a real Dixieland band would go highstepping it down Bourbon Street making the gladdest music they could, throwing a final party for the dear departed. "Nothing of the sort here in Boston, of course," he finished, and just as I wondered if there was a trade journal (*Today's Undertaker?*) to which he subscribed, we pulled into the lot behind the church.

Another strange moment: I found myself telling him thanks and good-bye as though we had just shared a cab from the airport, falling right in with his day-like-any-other-day tone. It took me a minute to remember exactly where I was, and exactly why, and where I was expected next, for the rest of the family would already be at Uncle Jack's by now.

Even so, I didn't go right away. In fact, I didn't go at all. Sat under the wheel with the motor running, possibly sat there that way an hour or more, I really don't know, though I did know every tick of the time how my absence would be viewed among the family. But clear pictures of Micky were coming at me now, snapshots, mixing the early times with some more recent. My God, this was a guy whose diapers I had changed. Who I had walked to his first day of kindergarten, holding his hand, and with whom I had grilled steaks just a month ago at my place, on the occasion of his thirty-fifth birthday. It was proving one hell of a confusion finding the right face for him, who had been a baby, a kid with wifflecuts, a longhair, sometimes a beard.

Finally I did ease out of the lot (stupidly, because by now I was crying) and started working my way through the city toward the Mystic River Bridge, awfully slow going on a Saturday. I just drove, spaced out and trancy, time and trouble of no particular concern to me. Between the beach traffic and the big race, the cars in Revere were backed up solid to Slade's Mill and by the time I crawled past the oil farm and pulled into the free lot at Suffolk, it was late in the day.

Later than I thought, actually, because there was no one at the turnstiles and inside I saw that the feature race, umpty-umpth running of the Massachusetts Handicap, was up in eight minutes. Much too late for study. I glanced at the entries and the latest odds, got in a line, and started ransacking my pockets for cash. It was pure chance that I had some.

Dixieland Band was held at 6 to 1, neither the long nor the short of it, but that didn't matter to me: if I got to the window in time to bet, he would be my horse—the undertaker's choice at any price. It was a close thing, too, as the character in front of me trotted out a lifetime supply of exotic wagers, triples and boxes and wheels. I grabbed my ticket as the machines were locking, the horses leaving the post.

By the time I was back outside and breast-stroking my way through the milling crowd to the rail, the horses had disappeared behind the tote board and the track looked strangely deserted, empty. With ten thousand fans screaming, the race caller was not much help; I hadn't a clue where my horse stood, or even what the hell he looked like. Then they came clear of the tote with a speedball loose on the lead. When I found my guy, though, the Dixieland Band, he was striding nice and easy off the flank of the second-place animal, and I felt a sudden wild surge, because I absolutely knew it was going to happen.

Right then he took over second, and as they turned for home he was rushing past the fading speedster and opening up a lead of his own so quickly on the straightaway that the late runners would never threaten him. Ten years away from the racetrack and here I was, still in the know, or so it felt until I remembered exactly how much expertise had gone into my wager. I had been given a horse, that was all, and by someone who hadn't put a lot of thought into the matter himself. We played the undertaker's choice, plain and simple.

The mutuel clerk was not a bit impressed when I went to cash. He ran my slip through the machine, slid two dimes my way, and then began licking off twenties like free passes to a religious meeting on the Common. His hands moved with the timehanging sameness, the strictly-business rhythm of a card dealer, and the bills flowed silently toward me as though they would flow forever.

Another race was already shaping up, but I had zero interest. It wasn't like I felt lucky, or like I even cared, win lose. I bought a couple of hot dogs, walked down to the bleachers, and sat eating my first food since Thursday. I wasn't thinking about Micky or anything else either, I was just buzzing it in the sun, eating hot dogs with mustard and feeling the warmth on my face, and maybe a little tingle still from the big strike. Dixieland Band were the only two words in my head.

The light had started changing, though, the crowd was draining away, and something told me I had better go soon, not linger, although I was not eager to jump into the crush of cars trying to siphon through the one narrow exit. Truthfully, I was loath to re-enter the world at all, through any channel. This ugly, unfamiliar bailiwick felt safe to me—nothing bad could happen to me here, not today.

Meanwhile I had forgotten all about him (and why I had come here, though who *knows* why) when there he was, my third-generation Harvard Porcellian undertaker, strolling from the clubhouse with a couple of well-fed friends. He wore a seersucker suit, faint gray stripes like regimented tinsel, and with his silver waves of hair he looked like the President of the United States at play, his two companions in their croc shirts and pastel trousers like Secret Service gone soft in the middle, thirty percent bodyfat on a good day.

We were crossing paths, as close as we had been sitting in his car, and I smiled; so did he. But as I started to speak he kept on going, for his smile had been one of instinctive politeness, not of recognition. Nor would you ever have guessed from his bearing that the man had just won a bundle of money, thousands of dollars I had no doubt. I trailed them out through the concourse, going three abreast; watched them into a valeted Cadillac at the curb, this one a dull canary yellow in the flattened light. He drove.

It was easy to understand his not knowing me. There were funerals every day of the week, morning and afternoon, and whatever they might mean to his relentlessly bereaved clientele, they could only be to him as melons to the greengrocer, or a pallet of two-by-fours to the sawmill foreman. Not that he had no care for them: on the contrary, he would do each one just right, perfectly if possible, and handle each account just so. Plus of course my eyes had been on him while his were necessarily on the road. All this I understood.

Even so I felt let down, abandoned, as I saw the pale Caddy make a calm clear line through the field of tangled cars. Because there was a magic about the man, there was special knowledge, such that he would understand *me* too. He would know why I was here at the racetrack when I should have been at my uncle's house, eating and drinking and mourning my brother who I loved so much. He alone could comprehend how on this day—this evil, numbing, desperately sad day—I had come to a place of frivolity and sin, and sinned with frivolous pleasure.

The Last of Harpo Berkowitz

Harpo Berkowitz had to be helped out of a car in Revere last month. He needed the help not because he was old or infirm, but because he was dead and it isn't easy for a dead man to get himself from the trunk of a car.

Okay, so much for the frivolous tone. I happen to be in the news business and that's just your story lead-in, what we call the hook or the grabber. The truth is I was the only sap in town who found the occasion of Harpo's passing anything *other* than frivolous. Because I chanced to know Harpo Berkowitz in high school, sat next to him in Cerasoli's homeroom from sophomore year on, and therefore exchanged pleasantries with him all those mornings. Were we friends? I was never sure, but I remember vividly and fondly that wide grin of his, the eyes almost closed like a cat's, and his admittedly wild ways.

Everyone else had him for a "hood," one full notch below the greasers in our outmoded social hierarchy. A greaser at least had his Ford to chop and channel or his Harley to gun and tune, whereas the handful of true hoods had nothing—possessions, sports, hobbies—and did nothing. They certainly didn't help to write the yearbook, as I did. I wrote the thumbnail for Harpo and I recall being impressed he still was *there,* getting fitted for a cap and gown. The others of his ilk (Zarillio, Zullo, the Kinney

Brothers, and Ralphie Flowers) were long gone, released by law on their sixteenth birthdays into the custody of outlaws. Gone to work in the world of chopshops, narcotics, and porno toys, or the relative dignity of the old daily numbers. But Harpo would wear the mortarboard, would shift a tassel with the rest of us, and I put in his squib: "Opera lover, savant, and gentleman-at-large. Looking ahead to a career in government."

To a great extent I was joking (or we were joking, since Harpo helped me compose the copy) yet he did have irony—he really was fond of the classic Italian opera. Harpo always carried himself with the air of a gentleman from some imagined Age of Gentlemen, an almost courtly manner that blended facetiously with the switchblade stiletto and the ducktail hair locked in grease, as did his habit of bursting abruptly into song with rich gesticulation and opera-house grandiloquence.

He was of course better known for acts of violence. Sudden, almost casual *tours de force* (but literal force) like the battle he fought one morning in the frozen school parking lot—with about five hundred kids looking on— against Rich Miller, the big football captain. Or the time he nearly decapitated Claude Thibeau, our autocratic shop teacher, with a three pound ballpeen. Those moments impressed me too, only differently, for I saw the smile, the mischievous grin that followed so quickly upon the apparently murderous impulses. It was not a psycho grin either; Harpo was all there. He was a joker, an ironist, with a feel for theater, or for the theatrical possibilities of terror.

Richie Miller towered over Harpo, and outweighed him a good forty pounds. They did not seem evenly matched as we watched them circle that cold morning, breathing plumes of vapor as dragons clashing might breathe fire.

There was special menace in the air, too, for here was a rare confrontation of cultures, of cadres that usually kept strictly separate—crewneck jocks versus the men in leather—and it seemed that something large was at stake.

For half a minute nothing happened, they just stalked one another clockwise (with Harpo's fixed grin appearing slightly lunatic under the circumstances) and then Miller unleashed a monster of a right-hand lead that brought a collective gasp from ringside. It made an audible rush in the crisp winter air. Harpo let it fly past his head almost contemptuously, his expression unchanged, then tackled the huge tight end and twisted his nose between two fingers until it snapped, again audibly, like a dry twig. The fight was over.

Afterwards in homeroom, your reporter was right there on the spot to interview the winner. "Good thing that right hand of his missed you," I began.

"Geesh," he scoffed. "You of all people ought to know better. A roundhouse job like that couldn't tag my mother in her sleep. That's what pissed me off."

"You were pissed off?" (I had to ask because he had never appeared anything but mildly bemused and distant throughout.)

"Sure I was. A showboat move like that? That's why I hurt the big jerk."

"What else could you do? It was you or him."

"That's true too," said Harpo, and nodded in consideration, as if to say the thought was new, but good.

"I always thought you had to be really mad to win a fight like that."

"Nah," he smiled. "Just dumb and mean."

Harpo did fire a ballpeen hammer at Claude Thibeau in the woodshop junior year. It rang off a cast-iron pipe about one inch portside of old Woody's skull, a hell of a fastball—Harpo surprised himself I'm sure. Certainly he surprised The Woodchuck, who turned back toward the workbenches in slow motion, like a statue revolving mechanically on a pedestal, his face white as flour. Harpo was already rushing forward, shaking his head in compassion. "Jesus, Professor," he said, "I am awful damn sorry, really I am. The damned thing just slipped on me and my goodness if it wasn't a near miss on you! Please accept my humblest apologies, Professor, I was careless. Careless."

Somehow it washed. The Woodchuck knew he had done it on purpose (in a way) and that the hammer had just missed ending his life right there in the high school basement. Yet Harpo disarmed him anyway, irresistibly, by combining that dangerous sense of fun with the uniquely self-mocking courtly manner.

So he was a legend of sorts: desperado decked in black (black pomaded locks of hair, black boots with the heavy silver buckles, tapered black slacks and the crackerjack black leather jacket too) who for the most part ignored this typecasting, who listened and laughed and sang snatches of his favorite, *Lucia di Lammermoor*. Often during our senior year I wondered what could possibly become of him. He really was too smart and too sensitive to be a street hood, yet it was hard imagining other applications for his particular genius. A bartender possibly, or a prize-fighter, though he was on the lazy side. An usher at the opera house, bowing the people to their seats and then standing in the back through all the great performances in his flowing black cutaway?

I asked him at graduation, the last time I ever saw him, what he planned on becoming. "A cowboy," he told me, with a smile as wide as the Pecos River. The wide white grin, the jetblack hair combed back in perfect lustrous parallels—that was Harpo, a cartoon chiaroscuro, walking talking contrast of means—and what in hell's name *would* he do, really?

What he did, ultimately, was get himself trunkstuffed in Revere about half a mile from where we graduated high school. No, Harpo had not gone far. Yet recalling his unique and stylish *persona* I found it hard to believe he had really gone *nowhere,* that he had become nothing more than a cheap hood after all, bearer of the black spot, bodyguard and gofer to whoremasters and drug tycoons. This was too cruel, too Darwinian a denouement. When the item came in from our stringer at the beach, no one in the newsroom batted an eyelash. Here was a non-story, just another "gangland slaying," the only kind of gory story that sold no papers. Even the modus was reheated hash, always the trunk of the abandoned car, that or the stoneboat in Davy Jones' locker. Nothing fancy, gents, just business as usual.

But I convinced Harry Eamon at the city desk to let me have two days on it. Might be a feature, I told him, because this one was special, the guy had real presence; he was a character and there would be people out there with colorful stories about him, people who loved and hated him. This one wasn't going to be Faceless Killed By Nameless but a human interest angle, What Really Happened To Harpo Berkowitz. I absolutely expected a story, a tragicomedy, and I also relished the chance to reel in the past, in the person of Harpo, to stroll down the road not taken and see what went on there. I never guessed it would be so quotidian.

His mother, for instance. Harpo used to mention her a lot, dammit, and always fondly. She was a great cook, I knew, made a meatloaf fit for kings. I had taken a chance with him that day, had contradicted him lightly: "Kings don't eat meatloaf, Harpo." "Nah," he shot back, at the ready, "they eat it all right, they just don't use ketchup."

His mother then, still alive in East Boston, still young for that matter at fifty-two, gave me a cup of coffee. She was a pleasant enough woman whose life seemed far from terrible. She was living alone in rented rooms but had a boyfriend, a car, and a steady job at the Prince of Donuts. She didn't look bad at all, not a drinker. But she did not feel so very maternal toward my old friend. "A bum," she summarized. "He got his."

I was stunned. "You knew him best," I said, sounding like television I'm afraid. "You must have known the side of him that was beautiful."

Her laughter came at me so sharply, so derisively, that I nearly ducked. Of course I had richly earned it with my purple prose. I hadn't meant to go sappy, but I was truly shocked by her venom and responded stupidly. "I haven't seen him, or talked to him, or *wanted* to see him or talk to him in years," she said now.

"He loved you very much," I said, still stupid, having not yet shaken the germ. I would have bet my last buck Harpo had been simply grand to his old lady—the generous and loving son if nothing else—and that she in turn would defend his name against all comers. He might have knifed the old man but he would absolutely reverence the mother, this much I knew. So much for Sigmund Freud and so much for me and my Reportorial Instincts.

"You been sneaking too much rum at your desk, friend. That kid was a gutterball from the cradle to the grave. A block of ice behind his lungs, where most people have some kind of heart. Harpo? Look, don't take my word for it, ask Cathy. Ask his wife."

His wife! The Harp Takes A Bride—impossible yet wonderful to contemplate. He had never looked at girls, not even the ones who chose to hang with the hoods, and there were more than a few. Not the prettiest ones exactly, the way you might see it told in the movies, but some with sex appeal and spunk. (Ellen Morrison, for my money, put all the good girls to shame.) Did not appeal to Harpo, however, or if they did he never showed it. It was as though girls stood outside his code, compromised him somehow. He did surprise me one morning when a new girl appeared in Cerasoli's homeroom; grinned at me and made the hourglass shape with his palms. Never before and never again such a reference as that, so I had him for a connoisseur, bloodless judge of talent who knew a good figure when he saw one yet disdained the hunt absolutely.

Now a wife. An interlude, at least, of normalcy and affection. If this Cathy had married him, she must have loved him, believed in him once and maybe still, despite the mother's surmise, for they were still man and wife when The Harp drew his last parking ticket out at the beach.

Cathy Berkowitz lived in an apartment five minutes' walking distance from the high school and once more I registered with some deflation that Harpo had not gone far. But it isn't all tinsel, folks, and whatever else you may hear in America today there is still nothing beats a true love and a strong close family tie. If Harpo had that, well then maybe he had done something unexpected after all. Which is why they say "if" is the biggest little word in the language.

Cathy hadn't seen his face in six years, which was inci-
dentally the age of their kid. And worse, like the mother,
she felt well shed of him, so low had she banked the fires
in her heart. The kid was named Kid—named like a fighter
I suppose, Kid Berkowitz—except he didn't look to be
much of a fighter. A dreary little sack of seed who, I soon
learned, had never met his progenitor, never even been
shown a picture. Having only just begun school, he might
not even know kids *had* fathers if not for the TV, where
come to think of it they often as not don't have fathers,
what with art mirroring life and all.

"I'm changing his name," Cathy told me. "From Kid,
I mean."

"To what?"

"If I had a good one, I'd done it already. But I'm going
to—both names."

"Last name too?"

"Cause now I can remarry, you see. I couldn't remarry
without a divorce and the son of a bitch wouldn't let me
have that cause then he'd have to pay me money. He was
smart and selfish to the end, Harpo."

"I'd change it as soon as possible if I were you. Once
they are in school, you know, the name gets locked in. I
mean the first name—" (I did not want to rush her on
the last name, having obtained the clearest conviction that
Harpo's mother would remarry sooner than his wife.)

"Any suggestions?" she said.

"Names? No. I kind of like Kid to be honest with you.
Or maybe Harp the Second. To me nothing else goes with
Berkowitz."

"You can say that again."

I went to the cops. It helps to be on the paper, so you know your way with them a little. There are two or three guys down there who don't give a damn anymore, meaning they might give a reporter the time of day. Virgil Lewis I would even call a friend—I'd stood him a few beers and vice-versa I'm sure—but Virge wasn't from these parts, he grew up out in Springfield. To him, the Harpo Berkowitz I described was a pure figment; he knew all about the real one.

"He was a punk, a delivery man. Really, that's it."

"A collector?"

"Probably a collector. He was tough enough."

"A trigger?"

"Can't be sure there. You prefer a yes or a no?"

"Not sure myself. But listen, he was big enough news to get his ass blown away, he must have been more than small beer to somebody."

"You think so? You think these guys are rational or something?"

I did. In a way, rational. Not your well-read scholar exactly, or your concerned citizen, but rational in the sense they would know the butter from the margarine.

"These guys are just terrorists. Lunatics with guns and muscle. Truly, this Berkowitz is not a story worth your time, anymore than a garbage collector, or a seagull at the dump."

I couldn't do a thing with the seagull. No story. Yet I was credulous to the end, because I *knew* this guy, and knew him not as an infant in his crib but at eighteen, with his habits and gestures shaped for life. There had to be more to it.

"Just one last thing, Virge, one simple answer and I'll get out of here. Who?"

"Who did him?"

"No. Well, maybe. Who employed him? Who'd he work for?"

"Hey, you want to end up getting yourself unpacked at the beach too?"

The salient thing with your modern-day syndicate man, the guy at or near the top, is this incredibly serious commitment to the idea of appearing normal. He wants to barbecue out back with the neighbors, get his kids into private school, go to the theatre with friends. He does his hardest work building up this normalcy front and one result is that you can find him, his telephone is even listed, although like anyone else normal he won't stay on the line too long with a stranger, least of all the Fourth Estate.

"It's about a dead man, you better speak to my lawyer," said Frankie Call, The Barge Man, who according to Virgil Lewis filed W-2 for Harpo Berkowitz.

"Believe me, it doesn't call for anything like that. I've got no axe to grind with anyone, I'm just trying to understand something. Come on, let me buy you a cannoli."

"Funnyman. What did you say you write?"

"Metro and County, Section Two. The human interest stories."

"Berko was human interest? I never even knew he was human."

"See, you're funny too. Come on, sir, give me five minutes. I'll drive to you."

"Oh, it's a favor you're doing me now, I'll save on gas?"

"You can always use a friend at Metro and County."

"Right, sure. All right, Jimmy Olsen Cub Reporter. Come to my house Sunday. Ten a.m., come around back to the pool. Bring a bug and you might get wet. Kiss your kids good-bye, just in case what they say about me is true."

"I don't have any kids."

"Kiss the dog, Olsen. I'm just kidding you, remember?—we're funny. I don't threaten people, I'm in real estate, I *deal* with people, a busy man, give you two minutes of my time."

"Three," I said, in case it was procedurally correct to bargain.

"One," said The Barge Man, closing the deal. But he sounded soft to me, the same way Harpo always had. Maybe they were all like that, full of the milk of human kindness with no way to express it except through the love of opera.

Call actually met me alone. Not really I'm sure; believe it, I was posing in somebody's crosshairs every second. I wasn't about to reach inside my jacket for a pen or a cigar, and even then I found myself hoping they didn't kill for mere sport on Sunday.

But he stood alone, slim and elegantly dressed in a brown suit, with the weary attentiveness of a parimutuel clerk. He looked down at my hand as though it was barely visible, certainly nothing to touch, then remarked that I looked "big enough to be a cop" and I told him I had a brother who was one, out in Sacramento. He said he didn't care, real estate men weren't afraid of cops. Then he made a nice little speech for me, with one wing-tip shoe propped casually on the diving board. (The truth: he was wearing Reeboks, same as me.)

"You want to understand life. All right, let's pretend I

know it all. Let's say I tell you a story about this fellow Berkenstall—is that the name you mentioned? I tell you he ripped off some goods wasn't his to rip off and so Billy The Q placed him inside a car for it, relocated him if you will. Say that Billy the Q was on retainer for such small chores as that and didn't even receive a penny candy for his troubles, where you guys are always writing ten thousand and twenty thousand and the sky's the limit. Now what if it was all just exactly that way and I knew it and told it all to you? Would it make you understand life any better? I'm curious to know."

His frankness blew me away. I was certain he had just supplied me with the literal scenario for Harpo's end. It was a show of absolute confidence in his normalcy front, as though nothing could touch him now, least of all reality. And I think he expected me to be entertained, amused, in any case satisfied—and to agree there was nothing to be learned, even with every fact in hand.

God knows why he'd consented to talk in the first place. Maybe just to stretch out his own curiosity and daring, maybe to show his humanity (that although he rigged the dice he could still feel sympathy with the players in the game) or possibly he had a simple egoistic enjoyment of his own strong-arm charm and liked to roll the power off his palate with one foot up on the diving board. Whatever it was, was gone. By now—and it really was one minute— he bore an unmistakable look of retrospective surprise at his own munificence, that signalled a definite end to it. He was still as a waxwork and the air around him seemed terribly still; the unnaturally blue water in the pool did not move a molecule.

"Didn't you like him, though?" I asked, ignoring the

cues for silence, for I was after a different sort of accounting than the one he had offered.

"What's that?" The Barge Man snapped awake, startled to find me there fully thirty seconds after he had stilled the water.

"Harpo. That's what I really wanted to know. Did you like him, personally."

"Like a son," he blandly assured me. "If I ever met him."

And that's about the whole itinerary, every place I went and everyone with anything to say, the complete wrap-up on Harpo Berkowitz. I have omitted such memorable stops as the one I made at Pete's Eats, where Harpo took his ham and eggs every morning. Asked for a word or two, an anecdote, the handful of regulars could barely muster a shrug among them. Needless to say I had no story. Nothing, said Harry Eamon, could be less of a story, and so I spent a month down on the South Shore covering polluted water as a penance, notes and quotes on coliforms.

Harpo Berkowitz was never so prosaic. Was I going too far to see him as an artist?—one whose discipline happened to be force, or terror, and who like so many artists in other disciplines had done his best work early on and was doomed to a reiteration of the themes? It was not a line I'd try on Harry E., who would call it a crock and a half before he hit the first comma.

So the morning line held: Harpo would go down as a punk, who had lived and died the pre-ordained life of the punk. A guy whose own mother despised him, whose only talent was that fearless existential muscle we had seen in the parking lot, in the woodshop, and once in the hallway outside the school cafeteria when The Harp came up on two pretty big boys and smilingly cracked their skulls together like cocoanuts.

"Your friend is deranged," I was informed by one of the cocoanuts that day, referring to the detail that he neither knew his assailant nor had provoked him in any way. "He's no better than a rabid dog."

Harpo himself recalled the moment for me a day later and having had the leisure to sleep on it, he did so with a gentle, almost wistful pride and pleasure. Certainly he was not chagrined that the act had been gratuitous. "I always wanted to try that," he drolly confessed, "and those two were born to be the ones."

The Street Where You Live

It is hard for me to ignore Frank Barlow, the tall handsome man who sits down in our street and wails there like a forlorn captive animal. The sounds he makes are inexact, not language, although bits of English do emerge from his inner music.

But here, I'll tell you what I know of the man. There are days when he limps terribly or even crawls along the curb, and yet it is perfectly usual to see him later the same day going along at a brisk pace, covering miles. He does cover miles every single day (the same miles, over and over) to no discernible purpose beyond the motion itself. Relentlessly tracking his private demons, I guess: downtown, back up to the river, across the railroad bridge both ways, then downtown again. We happen to be on his route.

I have seen him sleeping at night, in Trapelo Park and in the dimly lit foyer of the Harry S. Truman high-rise, but Frank is mostly on the move. Movement is his calling now, whatever it may have been before. And I should mention the rituals—unbuttoning and buttoning his coat, plus a kind of ceremonial unloading and repacking of his gunny sack that approaches autism in the simple pointless repetition. Much of this behavior is entered in the record, by chance, near our front steps, but it's the stuff we *don't* see that really fascinates. Frank has a lawyer, Frank cashes a monthly check.

He will never meet your eyes. If his path bodes a geometric intimacy with your own, he will veer, early and gracefully. He can see trouble coming, in other words, or society coming, I suppose. Speak and he will pretend he hasn't heard you, though it's always possible he does not hear, in one sense or another. It's as though a shell, a bubble, has been cast around him and yet he has this lawyer, cashes a check, eats.

You see, I have become peripherally involved with the question of Frank Barlow, who knows why? Plenty of others have managed to look the other way. To most of them, Frank is at best an unsightly reminder and at worst a frightening apparition from the downside of the American Dream. He is what can happen, what *has* happened, and he is right there in your face every day. "Too damn *bad* it's a free country!" I heard one neighbor say, as if he'd rather they kept Frank under a rock somewhere.

One assumes Frank is unhappy. It would be difficult to project any positive emotions onto his quirky ceaseless ramble, other than to note that he does ramble, and maybe that alone indicates hope. Maybe he believes instinctively he is "getting somewhere," whether to a good place in his past or something better on up the road. But I feel certain Frank would not want to be kept under a rock, because even on its most elemental level freedom itself is clearly what he loves. Movement. In this regard he is a true American.

Guessing his age at forty, one considers the possibility he coughed up his sanity in Vietnam; he may be a damaged veteran and therefore that sort of "true American" too.

It's not unlikely, though it does not quite jibe with one prominent and intriguing fact I have learned about Frank Barlow, namely that he is the son of wealth—the Barlows of Beacon Hill, no less. This I found out firsthand the day I rescued him from the snowbank last winter.

I almost left him there. It was just Frank after all— the familiar layers of shabby blankets, the battered brown shoes—except that I saw bright blood shining on the snow by his ear. Snowchips stuck to his beard and lashes, and even with his eyes shut he wore a look of terrible anguish. His fist unrolled and I saw a crumpled note. Rosebud? No, there were two names and two telephone numbers on the sheet, Attorney Ben Chasen and Alice Barlow, the Beacon Hill society woman.

Everyone knew about the lawyer, for that detail surfaced whenever someone sought to have Frank removed from view. I suppose we knew he had a mother, too, but not really—and not anyone like an Alice Barlow. From her public image, it seemed as unlikely she would have a child as he a mother, and *highly* unlikely they should each be such to one another. Yet they were.

I called the ambulance first that day, of course, then Chasen and Mrs. Barlow, leaving messages with functionaries of each. Chasen phoned that night to thank me. "It was thoughtful of you to call Frank's mother," he said in rather a warm voice, as though he mistook me for a family friend, or else for a second forgot I existed at all and was just talking to himself. But when I tried politely to further my knowledge of the situation, how things stood with Frank, the curtain came down quickly. "He'll be fine," Chasen told me. "In fact he has already been released from hospital and it's largely thanks to you, Mr. Glazier."

Frank was "fine"—that was his situation. Client confidentiality, and perhaps simple good manners, forbade my knowing more. But wasn't there another point of view? If this man was going to hurl himself upon the mercy and charity of the community, as a vagabond wanderer, intruder in the dust of our streets, would it not help those few who were sympathetic to him if they could know the nature of his difficulties?

Thus I retained the unlisted number and tried several times to reach his mother, identifying myself in diminuendo as a friend, as someone who knew her son, someone who had helped her son, someone. The functionaries stood firm. When a gift arrived for me in the mail (a gold wristwatch, with a note card, "In appreciation of your help, best wishes") I knew Alice Barlow would not be coming to the phone. Short of attempting to bribe the downstairs butler, I had reached a dead end there.

Naturally I tried approaching Frank directly, too. This fellow had a lawyer, and a mother, and he bought coffee and doughnuts at Winnie's Spa on the corner of Columbine and Orchard fairly regularly. True, he negotiated the purchase in silence, but I knew he *could* speak and one morning left the spa with him. "So, Frank, have you recovered all right from your fall? When you fell in the snow last week?"

Not a flicker of acknowledgement.

"I was the one who found you—I phoned for the ambulance. That's how I knew about it."

Come on, Frank, you *owe* me—that's what I was really saying. A word or two, a sketch of how things stand, a little something to go on. And this time I got a sort of response, a brief twitch, a cringe, as in a man with a hornet at his neck, folding away in self-defense. I let him go down Columbine alone with his breakfast.

That night I told my wife Rachel it was not worth the trouble, and she readily agreed; she had never thought it was worth the trouble, though not because she lacked sympathy for this poor soul. Wherever Frank Barlow was lost—whether in childhood, in Vietnam, inner space or outer space—Rachel was sure he was lost all on his own. Where no one could reach him.

Then two days later he was standing on his mark, below our front stoop, buttoning and unbuttoning his mackinaw. By the third run-through I was down the stairs with a plate of Rachel's famous molasses cookies.

Tess Browning, down the block, had fed him once. Fed him every morning for a month, that is, out her back door like a Thirties' hobo. Sandwiches and cartons of milk. One time he handed her money, as though she were running an eating club over there. Bizarre transaction all around. Tess never got a word out of him, never saw a smile, yet she believed he was glad of her caring, and clearly happy to eat. "But it was so strange," she told me, "to ask him what he liked—you know, tunafish versus ham-and-cheese, toast or on a bulkie roll?—and him with those bright faraway eyes just keep chewing."

Frank bolted from her porch the day he heard a telephone ring inside the house. Like a dog jumping back from a firecracker, she said. He was gone by the time she returned and he never stopped by again. Tess figured he must be on the lam, wanted by the police, or possibly a mental patient strayed off the reservation. But no: he has this lawyer, cashes his check. So he had run for other, more personal reasons, reasons stronger than hunger, as was pretty obvious every day of his life.

The cookies were no more than a pretext, a transition

from nothing to something; maybe they would hold him a few extra seconds. Plus, I had timed my arrival halfway down a placket (three buttons done and three buttons un) so he would be checked by that detail, too, and stay to hear me out. Such was my reasoning, at any rate.

Wrong. Stronger than hunger, stronger than autism or whatever it was that set him in pursuit of those buttons, stronger than my will to know was his will to be unknown, and to get clear of all situations. I had barely spoken ("Frank, my name is Frank too—") when he was off and hobbling, like a turkey through the corn, down St. James to Norfolk, his usual route but triple time, dual exhaust. I might have been fool enough to follow after him had I not felt fool enough already, standing in the street with my cookies. At least I had what it took to bring the neighborhood pigeons bliss. I have known two very specific insanities in my time: the crazy man who needed to kill pigeons, and the crazy man who needed to feed them. Now I knew which one I was.

No doubt my profession—a lifelong high school English teacher—made my next approach inevitable. Frank Barlow was alert and keenly self-interested; the problem was simply that his self-interest lay in safety, apartness, privacy. He would never stand still for talk, yet might he not accept *written* communications? Read them at his leisure and respond in kind? It might in fact amuse him very much to do so!

My first note was brief and to the point. "Would you care to correspond?" I wrote, and I took it to him at the bench in Trapelo Park where he often drank his coffee. I never even broke stride: dropped the envelope beside him (his name in red letters as clear as his blood on the snow that December day) then watched him from a distance. But it was like watching the Red Sox bat in a critical situation, it had that awful combination of caring and help-lessness. Get a hit! Read the note! No such luck.

If he had any human curiosity in him, his was a monk-like discipline. Was it possible he hadn't seen it? Or saw it but took it for a leaf, or a shoe, or a dead moose? The man did have his own reality, after all. But I had mine too, and gave him the note twice more ("Would you care to correspond?"), once outside Winnie's and once by the railroad tracks at dusk. Each time he allowed the communiqué to fall from his hand, or from the space between my hand and his, really. Let it flutter to earth like the discount coupons dealt out by shills at an indoor mall.

"Please, Frank," my wife advised, "this is starting to upset you more than you know." But I was pretty much convinced anyway—Frank Barlow did *not* care to correspond. It is to receive mail, after all, that we undertake to write and send it. If he had no interest in the incoming, what incentive could he have for writing back?

"Write back! Oh you poor dear, you've really lost it, haven't you," Rachel said. "You thought he'd write *back*? I thought you just wanted him to eat your cookies. *My* cookies, I should say."

Maybe because I really was ready to stop trying, he finally did respond, albeit in a dream. I say "a dream" and yet I wish you to understand the occasion could not have been more substantial, more real, had you been filming it live and in color on the street where you live. This was so vivid that I knew he had actually said it, or thought it—that it truly was his response being transmitted to me. Magically, telepathically, whatever. I do not believe in much (New Age, old age, nothing really), I am ye of little faith personified, but this was not something to believe or disbelieve, this was almost tangible.

We met on a bridge, or on a huge split tree arched over a fast stream, like the one where Robin Hood jousted so merrily with Little John and Friar Tuck. There at the midspan, as if by assignation, Frank looked me squarely in the eye at last (the tangled hair and sodden beard, the sad hollow eyes, but organized and forthright) and spoke two words: "Why me?"

I turned and left. Clearly I had come for his answer, as a courier, and could now return with that answer to my encampment, my superiors. Why me? That was the message.

But what did it mean to him? Here one saw some ambiguity, for the obvious interpretation—why had God singled him out for suffering—was so out of keeping with his mien, as a man who asked nothing and took the world's best shots every day. So perhaps he was addressing the question to me, asking why *I* had singled him out, assailed him. What did I hope to accomplish? And this possibility necessitated a second brief note, sent care of Chasen, in which I could offer up only the most tattered of bleeding-heart clichés: "Because you could use a friend, as who couldn't. Someone with whom to speak, even when it is difficult . . ."

Oh I know I'm probably wrong. I have been pretty consistent in that regard. Frank probably does not need a friend. I have few enough myself, true friends, and my truest, Rachel, has been giving me the strangest looks lately, as if she fears I may have caught the disease, and might prove a danger to the children. She has complained of my appearance, the beard, even though when I wore one years back she begged me to keep it. "I was used to it," she says. "All right I *liked* it." Not this time she doesn't.

You can live without friends, I suppose, and without communication for that matter. As for Frank, he treats me the same way as before, the same way he treats everyone; as if we had never stood together above the rushing water that late spring evening. Does he remember speaking out? Who knows? Who knows if he recognizes a face, or realizes I am the man who handed him mail, who spoke to him, who saved him. Who knows whether he sees a face *as* a face; one is only ninety percent certain he can see at all.

Well, I tried. Had I never tried with the man, I might have felt guilty, especially after fate assigned me to pull him from the frozen snow. So there may be no satisfaction, no resolution, but neither is there guilt. I am innocent. I may not even feel innocent, yet it can still be a comfort knowing that I *am*. Not guilty. I too could say, Why me, why was I singled out. Rachel has said it ("Why did it have to be you obsessing over that poor sick man?") as though the suffering were mine, or hers.

She talks to me, she'd answer any mail I sent her, but even after sixteen years of married life communication can sometimes be a real thornbush. Let's face it, we have our different ways of seeing the world, different names and weights to assign its objects and ideas. Why should she be so surprised by that? Why should I?

Catherine

It was May in New Orleans, but on a Tuesday night the jazz was soft, all the party girls seemed sleepy. Dean was just walking the streets when he paused in the alcove entry to a place called The 10-Spot. Inside, not twenty feet away, was a naked lady in a hammock above the bar.

An angled mirror duplicated her by parts—two heads of curly black hair, four white mounds of her backside, two of her four sandalled feet touching at the toe—the idea of which imagery was to make you stop and think, more or less. Even without the mirror, though, Dean might have stepped inside.

There were a number of girls (10 OF 'EM ★ EACH ONE A 10!) and they took turns, first in the hammock and then dancing on the leather tabletops. The first one was his, not for how she was or where she was so much as *who* she was. He even managed to catch her name from the barman and it seemed to him a small hoard of magic that he possessed it as she went about her business feeling anonymous and free. Dean tipped her five dollars after her first dance and she roughed his hair in thanks; now, he thought, she was aware of him too, they had a sort of relationship.

"Would you care for something to drink, sir?" she said, when she got to him. She had the look of a devilish child, dark-haired and lean-figured, with a playful southern rasp in her voice.

"Not just yet."

"You have to," she confided, leaning so close he could smell her body. "I mean they won't let you stay if you don't buy one."

"Okay."

"I'll bring you a beer, how about, and then you can just hold hands with it as long as you like, see? If you aren't yet thirsty, I mean."

"Sure." Her breath, riding on the lovely catch in her voice, was sweet like grass.

She took other orders, and other tips that were a lot larger. A tall shambling man in a baggy suit gave her twenty dollars and placed his two palms right on her bare hips. Catherine laughed and moved his hands away absently, as though she were taking a pan off the burner while tending the children. Waiting at the bar, she dropped sliced fruit in one drink while the barman drew beers, then delivered the round and disappeared into a back room. A willowy black woman rolled down from the hammock to dance, in bright red shoes and matching pasties. The man in the baggy yellow suit offered her fifty dollars for the pasties if he could personally remove them. She winked and pulled back at the last second, but it only made him clap and shout.

Dean was just waiting for Catherine to come back, hoping there weren't really ten of them, feeling anxious she might be done for the night, gone out the back. There was a redhead in the hammock now, her hair bleached the color of brick, and the clock showed five of eleven. The black dancer looked mad when Dean gave her a dollar.

Finally, at twelve, Catherine came back out and climbed

into the hammock, where Dean thought she might be falling asleep. Then suddenly she vaulted down, and stood at the jukebox punching in her personal tunes. She might not be the prettiest in a glamour way, but there was a quality in Catherine that made everyone quiet. She looked as though she had just gotten out of bed with no time to brush her hair and the electricity of the sheets still clinging to her. She didn't smell at all like soap or deodorant or perfume. She moved with unthought grace, like an athlete practicing casually in the sun with no one watching.

As her second number came shuffling up from the jukebox, she unstrapped her sandals and slid them right to Dean for safekeeping and if that didn't prove it she finished with a split that was all for him, her front leg sliding straight at his chin. Her eyes had a dark shine to them, like the surface of a lake at night. He locked eyes with her and hooked a sandal onto her big toe, as if he were part of the act. This time she came around to him last:

"You're not going to tip me *again*," she said.

"I am, though. Have to. You're the whole show."

"Damn it's hot in this place," she replied, taking the bills. "I feel like running through the streets instead."

"Come on, let's go."

Unthinkingly he touched her, a come-along gesture, and felt the thin sweat on her back. His palm slid down to the swell of her buttocks and rested there. She had his other hand, and the money, in both of hers, but he could tell that her hands were about to pull free. "That would be good," she said. "The two of us bare bum on Bourbon? But you see, sugar cookie, I'm on the ole time clock here."

"I forgot that. Forgot you were working, I mean. You seem so much at home, you know."

"I do like to dance."

"Dance with me later, then. After."

"*After,* darlin', is four in the morning. That's when they roll up the street and carry it inside."

"Tell you what, then," he said with a gentle proprietary pat on the shoulder. "I'll be back for you at four. It's a date."

Back on the streets of the district, Dean had a chance to be amazed at himself. He had known himself a long time and the Dean he knew was reliable, shy, dull—the last man to speak his mind directly to any girl, much less a naked showgirl. When he returned to The 10-Spot at four, the alcove was dark; one fluorescent deck burned over the bar, and two black men sat under it sipping gin. There was a six-pack of Dixie Beer in the hammock now, another in the mirror above it. A lean fellow with a long pocky neck, the hound from outside, told Dean to forget it, they were closed, but then Dean mentioned Catherine's name: "Why didn't you say so? She'd be back there getting changed."

He went through the door but it was just a wide hallway and all the dancers were half dressed, so he turned. She came chasing straight after him, cussing mildly as she buttoned her shirt.

"What are you doing here, you damn lunatic?" She rushed him out onto Bourbon Street, where the jazz was still winding faintly through the night, clarinets and trombones twining together like vines around the trumpet. "I can't believe you showed up here."

"You didn't want me to?"

"Never gave it the ghost of a thought, hotshot. I figured we were joking around."

"Why?"

"What do you mean why? What in hell ever made you

think a person could waltz in here and pick me up like that? Not to say at four in the morning."

"I never picked you up, Catherine. I asked you out."

"And I never said I'd *go* out. Anyway, how come you know my name?"

"Dancing in your bare feet is part of it—why you are so sexy and the rest not, I mean. I thought about that. It's like you're someone at a party, you know, just enjoying yourself. There's nothing phony."

"How in hell's name is a person going to be phony," she suddenly laughed, "in the total nude?"

"That's when it's easiest, I think. Just look at those other girls—"

"And what in hell's name am I doing standing here and *arguing* with you about it? How *do* you know my name?"

"I heard it in there," he shrugged. "Come on, I want to look at the river with you."

"Oh now I know you're certified. It's spooky as anything down there—dangerous too. And I still haven't said yes to a single word of this."

"Come on, Catherine, I didn't ask you to marry me or anything. You could say yes to a moonlight stroll."

The wharves were completely deserted and the vast, wild Mississippi seemed to command the whole city. Even in the sheltered locks, it was miles wide, brown and foreboding. The moon sat low and round above the opposite bank, highlighting a thousand contrary tides and swirling eddies. Wind flew back and forth among the warehouses, bouncing in the cold shadows between gigantic containers and stacks of pallets.

"It is spooky down here."

"Like I said."

"Cold, too."

"I'm frozen solid," she said and he took her hand. She gave it, then took it back. "I sure hope you aren't a murderer, cutie pie."

"Not nearly, Catherine. I love you."

"That is *awfully* stupid. You are either the saddest con man ever or your elevator stops two floors from the top, I honestly can't tell which."

"You can't tell how much I like you?"

"Oh golly, lots of folks do. That's what happens when a girl takes her clothes off. Men *like* you."

"Are you really cold?"

"Is a Frenchman really French? Bone tired too, if you can believe such a thing."

"Well let's go, then."

She led the way, through streets Dean had not seen before, but he had the odd sensation of being in charge, of leading in the other sense. To Dean this whole night had the quality of fate: that explained how it could still be happening. He held her tenderly around the shoulder to try and warm her. Eventually they stood at a locked iron gate, not far from where they had started walking, in the district.

"Could I stay the night with you?" he said.

"Oh and what'll you tip me for *that?*" she said, surprising him with her emotion. She'd been playful, tired, distant, maybe amused; now she looked angry and tearful just under the surface of her face. Dean had not been sure exactly what he was asking, but he had been sincere and could make no sense of her sudden touchiness.

"Is fifty dollars all right?" he said, wishing he knew exactly what she wanted him to say. Catherine looked so shocked he was sure he had blundered.

"I know it isn't nearly enough, Catherine," he scrambled ahead. "I just don't have a lot of cash—I never planned on this. But I'll write you a check. Will you take a check? You can *name* it on a check."

Her face changed, and changed again during his misguided try at decency. In the end she seemed to like him again, or feel sorry for him—whatever it had been before.

"Two thousand dollars," she said. "We take Visa and MasterCard too."

"Sure you do. Be realistic, Catherine." He held his checkbook in his left hand, fountain pen in his right.

"Okay, I'll be that. What do you do?"

"Pardon?"

"For work. For a living."

"Oh. Sales. I sell sporting goods. Not here, though. Up in Little Rock—outside of Little Rock."

"All right then, let's make it for two hundred fifty, why don't we."

Dean never hesitated. He wrote the check and handed it to her, and they passed in through an earthen courtyard to a door which Catherine unlocked. Then four flights of spiralling ironwork to a balcony hung with blue and yellow flowers and another door. She let them into an airy studio room and pulled a string to light it. He liked the room immensely: a huge mattress under tall windows filled with dawn sky, bright posters, candle lanterns, paperback books, and clothing strewn over wooden furniture. This was her all right. His heart moved clean and quick, he felt incredibly happy, as though for the first time ever he was a person who could choose his own dreams and just live them.

"I better poke in and make sure my old man's asleep," she whispered, a stunner that really caught him but only a joke, she reassured him with a quick laughing touch. Then she began getting comfortable, settling in, disregarding him completely. She listened to messages, went through her mail. Dean watched her intently, as he had earlier, and though he recalled the glisten of her skin, the smooth hollow of her flanks, he was just as rapt at the sight of her clothed, and still. Her face was prettiest, he decided, when she smiled, but also when she frowned her doubt.

"I really do like you," he said.

"I thought you loved me," she casually reminded him, as she was yanking off one shoe.

"I really believe I do."

"As well as you know me."

"I believe you like me too. Bet you never took a check before."

"I never did take one before."

"Well the check is good, Catherine. Absolutely."

She slid her pants off and draped them over the gray-green face of a TV set on the floor. Bending, she pulled two shirts off in one motion and flung them in a tangle across the room. She stood naked and laughing as she ripped his check in two. Was the deal on or off?

"So do you love a lot of girls?" she said.

"Absolutely not. Only you."

"But you do have a wife."

"I can't lie to you, Catherine."

"I don't think you can, sugar cookie, and there is no need to either. But listen here, it's sleep time for me and I guess you are welcome to do the same on one condition—snore once and you're gone. Shake on it?"

Catherine looked sweet and drowsy under the skein of black curls. He could not imagine a minute of life without her; could not believe he would really be back in Galloway ten hours from now. But apart from the handshake she offered, he didn't touch her. "I'll cook you breakfast in the morning," he said.

Dean slid in alongside her underneath the cool sheet, thinking, This could be a dream, an actual dream, how would I know? Even if Catherine, already deep in sleep, woke and came right to his arms, it could still prove out a dream. But she won't, he thought: won't wake, doesn't want me, doesn't even know I'm here.

Shaking hands he had noticed a bracelet, or rather a blue rubberband worn as a bracelet. So she had never been completely naked until now, when he slipped it off her wrist. At this point, with sunlight dimly seeping into the alleyway, it was darker inside than out. Across the room, the silhouette of two slices of toast peeked up from an old toaster, the kind with rounded corners. Dean, who couldn't even try to sleep, stared at the toast and the blooming sky behind it.

A truck was cawing its backup warning below as he dressed. He wrote the words with a crushing sadness on his chest—I will always love you—knowing she would only be amused, not believe it, not care, but also knowing it was true. Then he came back, laid a five dollar bill on the note and added, This isn't money, Catherine, it's the breakfast I owe you. Love, Dean.

Doing that made everything better. He smiled going down the spiral stair, smiled through all the sunny cluttered streets to the hotel, and it was good to smile again. Now she had his name and could keep it, the same way he would keep the rubberband: as proof, innocent and ordinary, that fate and dreams were often less so, yet no less real.